GOD FORGETS ABOUT THE POOR

ALSO BY PETER POLITES

Down the Hume
The Pillars

GOD

FORGETS

ABOUT

THE

POOR

PETER POLITES

ultimo
press

Published in 2023 by Ultimo Press,
an imprint of Hardie Grant Publishing

Ultimo Press
Gadigal Country
7, 45 Jones Street
Ultimo, NSW 2007
ultimopress.com.au

Ultimo Press (London)
5th & 6th Floors
52–54 Southwark Street
London SE1 1UN

    ultimopress

 A catalogue record for this
book is available from the
National Library of Australia

God Forgets About the Poor
ISBN 978 1 76115 164 4 (paperback)

Cover design Amy Daoud
Text design Simon Paterson, Bookhouse
Typesetting Bookhouse, Sydney | 11.75/19.25 pt ITC New Baskerville
Copyeditor Camha Pham
Proofreader Rebecca Hamilton

10 9 8 7 6 5 4 3 2 1

Printed in Australia by Griffin Press, an Accredited ISO AS/NZS 14001
Environmental Management System printer.

 The paper this book is printed on is certified against the
Forest Stewardship Council® Standards. Griffin Press holds
chain of custody certification SCS-COC-001185. FSC®
promotes environmentally responsible, socially beneficial
and economically viable management of the world's forests.

Ultimo Press acknowledges the Traditional Owners of the Country on which we work,
the Gadigal People of the Eora Nation and the Wurundjeri People of the Kulin Nation,
and recognises their continuing connection to the land, waters and culture. We pay our
respects to their Elders past and present.

Dedicated to Mina
and all those who God forgot.

PART 1

2021

BELMORE
HONOURED CITIZEN

Start when I was born. Describe the village and how beautiful it was. On the side of a mountain but in the middle of a forest. If we walked to a certain point on the edge, we could look over the valley and see rain clouds coming. Sometimes we would see a cat on a roof, we read that as a warning of a storm. When we looked down, we saw the dirt, which was just as rich as the sky. My island, your island, our island. It's named after the white rocks at the mountain peak. It's those same rocks that make the ground full of nitrate—a natural fertiliser. Set the story there, this is the geography, but start with the day I was born. Add salt and pepper and fat. Say the October rains were creating a fine mist on the day, that it turned the air to glass. That something in the weather was special. Make it magical in the way that artists do. You're supposed to be a writer, try and write something good this time. Be interesting!

Our villages on the island are hidden. Up winding roads, in recesses between mountains. Back in time it would have been harder for raiders and pirates to get to. People call them villages, but they are settlements. Made up of a series of neighbourhoods. It might have been that there was good shelter on the side of the mountain, or it was closer to good farming, so they congregated. Set up dwellings and such.

In those little neighbourhoods we kept each other safe. If a girl was approached by some tacky boy, some want-to-be bandit, the men might gather and visit him, have some hard words. Or sometimes the eyes of the village would watch from around corners and see that one of the families hadn't harvested enough before winter, give them some extra stores before they could ask. Much unsaid but monitored. Do you remember when we were there? That time you and your cousin went to the beach on the other side of the island? By the time you came back, someone else had told me where you were. That kind of safety, you can only get there.

What do you mean it's not interesting? People will want my story. My god. I sound like one of those wogs that used to come to the library asking where they could tell their story. You know, they publish their own books. But my story is unique. I promise.

I was born in the smoke of the world war. Tell them that. Guns and cannons going off in canyons as my mother let me enter the world. The exact place? A hospital? No, you fool. I came out of my mother in that same house we stay in every time we visit Greece. That—more like a hut than a house—place.

Two rooms only. Imagine me being born while bombs exploded all around. And the soldiers travelling up and down roads! I'm sure I was born there.

No, wait. I wasn't born there. It was another house that we were renting. There was an earthquake on the island in 1938. It demolished our family house, and your grandfather took way too long to rebuild. We rented near the school at the top of the village, and beyond it was a forest that was too close to foxes. Me and my sisters came out of our mother, five girls born and burning.

Your grandmother had just given birth to me. No such thing as a doctor up there. She got married at about twenty-seven, a very old maid back then. I was embarrassed by how old I was when I had you and your sister. There was a village midwife who caught all the babies. I remember her. She was a refugee from the Asia Minor Catastrophe. Came to the island after the big population exchange. Poor dear came without a husband, just her two children. When someone comes from war, you can't ask: What happened to your husband? You can't say: So, tell me about the hard war. She was a victory wife though. Oversaw the birth of all children in the village. How was she paid? Ha! When you ask of currency, I realise you don't understand. People weren't paid to be midwives back in those days. They did it because they were part of the community! There was a love of work, not for nation or glory, but because working in the community for your people is the value. She spoke Greek as a second language. Her first language was Turkish or Ottoman, Hun, or whatever.

Turko-Greeks are darker than us. Her sons were the darkest in the village. She was always swooshing around the place in her birthing smock. When we were born, our father might have given her a chicken or something but there was no official gift. I always thought she liked to bring life into the world. Balance from the war she came from.

It was customary not to pay for births because sometimes things went wrong. Back then, women died in childbirth all the time. You couldn't imagine it. My sweet mother—may God protect and keep her—was an orphan. Her mother died giving birth to twins. There was no one to take care of them in the village, so it was kinder to let the two babies die by her side. Technically they weren't baptised, so it wasn't seen the way it is now. According to the time it was all right to let those babies die. Of course, I'm shocked. Don't ask stupid things. Different time when your grandmother was a child! No one to take care of two newborns. Could barely even feed the children that were alive back then. The eighteen-somethings, in a Greek mountain village. You couldn't even dream it.

See, it is interesting! You're not sure you want to write my story for your next book? All Holy, listen. You can't keep writing your gay things. And a son writing a story about his mother is not a gay thing.

People like books about war. At the library, most people borrowed books on war and romance. The first part of my life was in a world war, then in a civil war and I have had no luck in love. People will love my suffering.

I have some memories of war violence. I remember being a child and walking into the village square and seeing bodies of dead men strung up on rafters. You know when you are young, sometimes you see things but don't understand how big they are. I was too young to understand what I was seeing then. Remembering it is like looking through tempered glass. Blood fell on village square pavements.

Sometimes I can remember being a young girl and I look down and I can see my legs. Both fully there. Both are working. The thighs strong. Each calf present. One isn't deformed like it is now. And I don't think I can see the bodies of the communists in my mind but there was a smell to them. You don't forget smells because your nose won't let you. I won't tell my grand-children about those memories that are in my nostrils. I will show them how to combine egg and lemon in a soup. And I will teach them how to make Greek words plural. And they can tease me about the way I pronounce 'O' in that racist way you did, but I will not tell them the truth about that time. I was always hungry, you understand. We had one meal a day. Stewed greens and fire-toasted bread. You couldn't even imagine. We had to glean and forage dinner from fields and forests.

During the civil war, our village was communist. Your dad's village was more right wing. All seaside villages seemed to be. They were on the south side of the island. They were more exposed to the elements, to raiders, to Italy. They needed that big masculine protection that comes with armies and structure. Or, you know, sometimes living next to the ocean just makes you conservative. Like the people in Australia. Must be the slow way the waves hit the rocks and make them change. Must be the way the economy worked down those places. Up in the mountains we were more autonomous but we all had to work together. You know it was us mountain dwellers that won the wars against the foreign invaders? It was our guerrilla tactics and understanding of the terrain. You know your uncle through marriage? His mother was one of the Reds that fought off the foreign invaders. She told us a fable to keep us in check. Said that a young man was murdered because he snitched on the communists. When that snitch was buried, the earth wouldn't accept his body. Spat him right back out and he turned into the undead. Do you believe it? We did. That same uncle? When he was a child, his job was to smuggle food to the guerrilla fighters. Ten years old, he did it—you couldn't do any of that. None of you Australian born could. You are way too baby. You would probably be dead if you were born when we were.

War is interesting to read and terrible to go through. At the library, everyone loved that Captain Corelli book. One of the girl characters was called Very Foreign. Same name as my sister. When I told my big sister that there was a character in a book named after her, oh my god, a smile grew across her face. People love that. Another war thing you could do is write the story that your father tells everyone. About how he hates one of my relatives because they killed one of his relatives. Those pretty white cliffs aren't so pretty now, are they?

A woman's life is suffering and that's why we like to read suffering. Still not convinced to write my story? Why? Because it's a woman's story? Sometimes I don't think you're gay, I think you're just an extreme misogynist. Gays have no temperament for the suffering of women.

When us five girls were growing up, we never had trouble being slim—unlike you and your sister. That was a good thing about village life. Working in—what you would call—farm life. Where we worked our bodies. And then swapped things to live. Flour for ready-made Vienna loaves. Or sewing buttons for fabrics. Money wasn't the same thing that it is for you. Our lives were farming and then cooking over wood fires. Electricity? What was that? And for us girls, the five of us would go to school and then study afterwards. If we weren't studying, we would have to help around. Seasonally we would labour on the fields, shaking the olive trees and collecting the bitter pebbles. It kept us very slim. I never had problems with my weight, until you two grew up.

We should visit my older sister in Caringbah. You can hear her yap, yap, yap because she remembers me more as a child.

Back then, to have five girls was a curse. Perhaps there was a hex. I'm not sure about God, but you know me, how I skirt between believing and tradition. I still fast those forty days. You know I smoke the house out with the thurible. You know I sew up some sea-washed amulets. But even though to have only girls was considered a curse, we have a saying: Mothers that only have sons end up crazy.

We were three girls in a row. When I was born it was decided that I would be dedicated to one of the island saints, at his consecrated place. There was a monastery in the forest called the Cells of the Holy Fathers. It was founded by three holy men who set it up around the time the Empire changed to Christianity. The three founders came straight from The First Council of Nicaea and set up a place of worship in some caves. And they were so holy that even after they had passed my parents hoped the three men might amplify my family's prayers for a boy. We prayed to them so they could be a megaphone to God.

My family tried for a boy. But what is there to say. I can't talk about that.

When we were children, Open Sea—the eldest—had to solicit donations for the Cells of the Holy Fathers. She was young and had to go through the forest paths to those dedicational caves alone. It took about half a day to get there. Over rocks and moss, under the protective canopy. Then she would pick up a money box and the icon. She would come back through the forest. At the village she would hold the box and icon, showing the three men who had made the Cells of the Holy Fathers. After she received the donations, she would walk back, carrying that heavy box all the way through the forest in darkness. As we got older, we all took turns doing that. And I can remember returning the filled money box to the Cells. Carrying it through the forest path. The heaviness stretching my arms, creating an ache. The sound of the coins in the dark, like bells chiming as

I stepped over rocks. No one has pictures and sounds like that in their heads anymore.

Your own grandfather was devotional, a man from another time, though he just wanted to be a farmer. You know he worked the gendarmerie. The gendarmerie? They are like a kind of rural police force for farms. Found all throughout Europe. His job was to pass on judicially if neighbours were having disputes about a field. Or chase down bandits if they were coming through. In Greece, they get rotated around the countryside until they age out of it. That's when he arranged to be married. Just as his career was ending, he wrote letters to people he knew all around Greece and they arranged the wedding for him. A letter and his name got him married. That's an honour. Eighteen years difference between he and his wife. He was forty-five when he retired and got a pension for life. I think most of those men don't work all the way to the end. Some just get killed. One relative of ours ended up getting pierced by the arrow of love and he left his job to marry some old crone. So, the fact that my father stayed the whole way through means that he was a very disciplined man. He was someone that could go through hard things.

My father said he was politically neutral. But like most of those in the forces, he leaned right. Military and policemen seem to go right wing. But his best friend was that communist matriarch that organised the guerrillas. I think he publicly straddled both sides because he didn't want to lose his government pension.

I can remember him stinking like a farm worker when he picked us up from school. His hands had the black earth on them too, and at first I was embarrassed. But he was always asking us what we learned in school. I think he wished he could have learned with us. He respected books and words. Wanted to know more about them. My sisters and I were some of the few girls in the village that got an education. Our father insisted on it. Back then? Forget it. Most men wouldn't do such a thing. That's what my father has in common with your father. They both love education. Remember how unhappy your father was that time you came home from art school? And you told him that you were playing with a forge and he looked at you like you were an idiot? Because you are. He wanted you to have a real education. He is proud of his daughter though. With her three degrees. Even though he fears her and goes for months without talking to her. He still goes to the tables at Roselands and tells strangers about his daughter: The Lawyer! The Engineer! The Economist!

You and your sister are both mine and you don't care for your father that much. But you should love him, just because he is your father. There are other things worse than hitting. You know he would scream every time something went wrong. Sometimes he might not be here and I might drop a glass by accident and I can hear the screaming and shouting he might do at me. He screamed because he was scared. I've met his family. Let me tell you. They did things to him. He was such a scared man and vain too. Do you know he has these wardrobes that are just full of clothes that he never wears. Three wardrobes of crap.

Those loafers from Florsheim. All the suits that he had made for himself at Fletcher Jones. Oh my god, that combination of grey pants and blue jacket that he used to wear at events. When I see you do it, know it makes me want to vomit. That man has been horrible to me. Has suffered me. But you must love him.

This is a family I belong to. It's here in Australia which is now my home. I am happy to be put into the ground here. But there was another land whose soil I wanted to rest in. That village one. What do you want me to say about it?

Village life is finding already dead bat bones and getting them washed so they can be sewn into a keep safe. Village life is being in a forest and running past the cemetery so the undead won't rise. Village life is precarious and some family members would not have died if we were born rich.

People felt sad for my family in the village. Because we were five girls. We started to get those looks from passers-by. Side-head sorry looks. We didn't have time for them, but I know those looks. Mrs Katina gave me one when she found out you were gay and I would never have grandkids from you. As if I care. Or those 'oh sorry' looks that I got from Mrs Sophia when you went crazy and had to move back home. Like her son isn't insane from the steroids. Or the kind of look that Mrs Dina gave me when she found out that my daughter was going to marry a Xeno, a Jew. Like her daughter didn't marry some shepherd.

I look back on growing up as one of five girls. As children we walked to school and the neighbourhood boys would annoy us. Throw rocks or hoot at us while they were up in the trees.

When we were teenagers they would be more forward. One time a young man from the Three Roses rolled up to us on a motorbike and tried to engage us. One of us told our father. And he went straight to the family of the boy. They did nothing, said the boy had done nothing wrong, he was just talking. Then our father went to the local police officer. Because we didn't have a brother, he wanted it to be clear to everyone. Don't mess with my girls. He was vigilant.

He wasn't always so high-minded. Harmful stuff happened to the family and there was a change in your grandfather. He stopped caring about what people thought about him and the rules of what girls should be. It was one of the good things about having an old dad. He found wisdom in a way that many men don't.

You know my eldest sister, Open Sea? Your grandfather saw the deft way she mended socks and he made sure she trained as a seamstress. My god she could sew something good. When she came to Australia she was already married. She lucked out and found work as a seamstress. Found a job through the Redfern church. Earned more money than the men! She was doing skilled work! She deserved it! When they saw how much she was making, they were all angry. Men are weak like that. My god Open Sea was so proud of herself. She liked rubbing it in the men's faces. You imagine them, sitting around in their open shirts and their worry beads! Getting angry at the cafes! Ha!

And there was me. I liked learning and was good at maths. In high school I studied Shakespeare in French. Tell that to those who call us dumb wogs. I started a degree in Athens. Though I didn't have the support to finish it and I guess I got distracted with the way the world worked and looking for love.

Our youngest sister became a nurse. Worked her way through the union. Active in the communists too. And my god your papou got angry at her for being so active amongst the Reds. I don't think it was the politics. He was simply scared that any government might cut his pension. Few women were like us from that time and place. Many of the other women who came from the same places didn't do as well.

All our education was due to my father. Five girls. All educated. Unheard of at the time. And now look at the next generation, your cousins. All the women have two degrees! Two degrees each! Your sister has three. And the men of your generation? Well, at least they are handsome. Not you, your other cousins. Very handsome. Light skin, blue eyes and fit.

Of course, you don't know people's stories, especially those women that weren't supported to have an education. Why they did or didn't do well. And we shouldn't live in a world where the born lucky are more important than the born poor. We need to show respect to everyone. Especially the ones we don't agree with. I don't want cousin killing cousin again. Like the civil war. I'm not smelling blood again. Your father doesn't deserve respect, but you should still love him. And don't forget. How you tell the story is important as well. Remember, I'm a migrant too. People like stories about migrants. Most of the migrant stories are happy though. We came here on a boat, blah, blah. One suitcase in our hand, blah, blah. We came on the plane, blah, blah. We all sung a song about moving here, blah, blah. Rubbish.

Few of us realised that we came here to clean their toilets. This country tricked people into thinking that they loved multiculturalism. Made them think that this country was working. That this country was all right when it wasn't. When the woman Prime Minister lost the election? Remember what I said to you? I knew this country would never tolerate a woman prime minister, this is a country of misogynists, I said that to you.

The way this country doesn't understand women is the way they don't understand migrants. We have broken stories because a better life for us meant our hands were in factories but our hearts were agrarian. It was repetitive, folding up boxes and counting the right amount of chip packets in a box. You don't know what it's like to be in a factory. That kind of work does something to you. And we had this idea that we would make a better life for ourselves, that our houses would have big columns and a brick arch that went from the living room to the kitchen.

All the while I was here, I had this longing for another place, a past time that I didn't know was good. I still have that melancholic nostalgia. I still miss breaking the pine needles on my hand and then putting my nose on my fingers. I miss hearing my mother's voice, floating out of a kitchen window, asking me if it was going to rain. Then climbing the right mountain path, knowing which rocks to step on, and looking over the expanse of the valley for the right kinds of clouds that make rain—the ones that are flat and grey. I didn't know it then, but it was something else to see those clouds coming.

You should come to my house in the afternoon. There are these flowers that are blossoming. The sun hits them in the strangest places. The light explodes on their orange petals. When I saw them, I thought to no one, my son would like to see them. It reminded me of the small pieces of colour of my childhood. In the forest when the green wasn't enough sometimes. When I might find bits of white flowers and red berries.

I will tell you why you should draft my story. Because migrant stories are broken. Some parts in a village where we washed our clothing with soot. Some parts in big cities working in factories. How we starved for food in Greece and starved for Greece in Australia.

You don't know the first thing about me. A son can never see his mother as a woman. You will only see me in relation to you. I have had a thousand lives before you were even a thought. Hospitalised as a child for an entire year. Living as an adult without family in Athens when the colonels took control.

Living in Athens was something else. LA International Airport! I heard that song when I worked at the sugar patisserie. It played on the radio as I served customers. Oh my god the owner made us server girls wear these low-cut tops! The first and last time in my life. I'm not going to be like your sister. Wearing her low-cut tops and walking around as a lawyer! Remember when I saw her that Christmas, I was shocked at the dress she was wearing because I couldn't see her cleavage. First time for everything. I said that to her face and she got so angry. That song about the Los Angeles Airport? Same song came on the overhead speakers when I was on the plane coming to Australia. And then when I came here, working at that factory, I heard it there too!

I was happiest in Athens. At the time the colonels were rising. You could see all the army on the streets. Guns marching amongst the towers. But I was staying with our relatives. They weren't relatives but, you know, people who had kin connection through baptism. My father met them when he was stationed in the northern town called Drama. Only good people from there. You know mainlanders are good people, they aren't sneaky like us islanders. Our interfamily relationship started when he baptised one of their children. So then one of the Drama family baptised one of my sisters and then one of my sisters baptised one of theirs and so on. We weren't blood but chosen families can be better than your own.

The woman I stayed with was part of these Drama people. She became like my mother. A mother that I had in adulthood. And I connected with her so closely. You know she would kneel over me and mend my torn hemlines. And I would buy flares and cut my hair and she would tell me how fine I looked. She cooked for me, tried to find me a man. She had a young son. A boy in primary school. It was the first time in my life I had ever lived with a male. Like a child or little brother. I didn't know what to do with him except love. All children deserve love. You know, I went on dates. No! I won't tell you everything.

There were one or two suitors. But there was a rich man who rejected me, and your father still thinks that I love that man more than him. To this day he gets angry at me. Last week after a fight he accused me of still being in love with that same man.

That rich man rejected me and married someone else. But the woman ended up barren and couldn't have children. I was happy he suffered. Well, what? He broke my heart. Serves him right.

After that I came to Australia, and I was so unhappy. I used to sleep in my sister's living room and cry in the darkness. During the day, I worked in factories or looked after my nieces and nephews. I felt like no one wanted me around, overheard my own family complaining about me, so after a few months I packed up and went back to Greece. Went straight back to the island. That's where I met your father and we decided to come back to Australia. But this time we went to Tasmania. I picked him because, despite all those heartbreaks in Athens and Australia, I still wanted a family. I wanted children. It was the right thing to do, the natural thing to do. But that didn't turn out so well for me.

Your sister was the first baby in Tasmania to have the ultrasound on her. And while we were in Tasmania and I was pregnant, your father decided to teach me to drive. Wait until I tell you how he did it. He drove the Kingswood all the way to the top of Mount Wellington. And then he turned the car off and took the keys out. Put me in the passenger seat. Told me I needed to roll the car all the way down the mountain with no engine on. And then he just watched me do it and yelled at me when I did the wrong thing. I was seven months pregnant and so scared.

Your father wasn't with me when I gave birth to your sister. He called a few hours after. I told him over the phone that it was a girl and there was silence. Told me he was busy. He didn't come for three days. And we were in Hobart at the time, I had no family around me. Had some friends but Tasmanian Greeks are all running from the mainland. Exiles. Some of those friends came. They kept asking if my husband had come, when would he show up. There was silence when I said he was too busy. Made up excuses for him. But that kind of embarrassment, of your husband not showing up at the birth of your first child? Forget it. He said he had shifts at the Casino. For three days? Come now. But when you were born in Paddington? He sent two vases of flowers. One of them was a blue vase with blue flowers. Where do you even get blue flowers? He came to the hospital and handed out chocolates and cigars. Gave them to all the nurses, people that were walking down the hall, doctors that weren't even involved in the birth. I smiled and said, That's enough now! It would have been sweet. But he did nothing for his daughter so each gift that I saw him give made me bitter.

That man wanted you to be like him. Bad men have dreams for their sons and indifference for their daughters. They hope their sons will turn out like a version of themselves but not as good. Remember how he said he wanted you to work in bars and hotels like he did? Well, you do that now. But also, you are doing that writing. Don't forget all that writing stuff is all me. Those books are me.

Your father didn't want a second child. That's why I couldn't believe the way he acted at Paddington when you were born. That's right. You weren't wanted. Oh, get over it. You know this. We were only going to have one child. But I thought having another baby would be nice. I kept asking him to have another child, but he kept on saying no.

So, you know what I did? I got him drunk one New Year's. An extra dash of whisky here and there while we partied. That's why you are a Virgo. You know how long I smoked for when I was pregnant with you? As long as I had to. It was 1979. We all knew by then it was not good to smoke when pregnant. But I needed to hide the pregnancy from your father until it was too late. So I kept buying my packets of Holidays. Chuffing away. Oh, be quiet. Nothing wrong with your brain from my smoking. It's all the other stuff you put into it. All your drugs.

Oh, when I had a boy! What a joy. We were living in the back of a shop in Brighton-Le-Sands. Just a block down were dunes and sand. Even though there were shipping containers along half of the bay, it was still the beach. Still got that fresh ocean air. Round the corner was our family doctor. She was Irish. Divorced but still a good lady. Your sister was in kindergarten. She would come home with new things that weren't hers. Excuse me? Where did you get that eraser? Where did you get all those pencils? She said someone gave it to her. Bullshit. We got called to the school. She was stealing everything from the other children. We asked why she took the things and she said she just wanted them. Oh well. Shows her strength, eh?

That little mixed business we had was cute. I said we should start making and selling food. But your father spent too much time flirting with the female police officers that dropped by. For some reason he had a thing for those kinds of women. I was so embarrassed when I walked into the shop holding you and saw him act like that. We sold everything there. It was more like a mini supermarket. You were a peaceful baby. Never crying. Slept on time and ate. And I said to myself, Oh my! This is why the Greeks love boys! But then you ended up gay.

After you were born your father wanted us to move back to Vasiliki. It was all because of you. I didn't want to go, I wanted to stay here in Sydney. But I compromised and lived for a while in Greece because we had to baptise you there. The boy! The heir! The big masculine thing! Ha!

In Greece we went to live with his side. You don't know anything about your father's mother. That grandmother of yours. By protocol we had to give your sister her name but the only thing they share is determination. She never loved. I don't think she could love right. Greeks can't say horrible things about the dead. But we do it anyway and then say God protect and keep her. She was a horrible woman, a terrible mother and possibly a witch. May God protect and keep her.

You were thirteen months when we lived with her at that seaside village. The locals from the other villages called that place the hole of the island. I think it was cursed. Tourist money made some people's lives better but not ours. It was still a hole and I never liked making you live there. In a house with rooms in it like an afterthought. Your sister was a few years older than you. My god you were both smart. Your dad is smart too. But you both learned from me. I spoke to you in Greek and English. So you ended up speaking so late. Your first words were at three years old. Like when you called for water you would say the Greek word first and then the English word. Nero/Water. Nero/Water.

It was nineteen-eighty something and we were scraping money here and there. I was tutoring English, but your father wanted to be a farm man. He would fix things. Build fences. Tend to the animals. We had goats there, two cows, and I think there was a donkey. This was the eighties, mind you. Who wants to live like a farmer in the modern age? My two older sisters had businesses and washing machines and chlorinated pools. And we were stuck on an island. Water and electricity went on and off. And we had to live with your grandmother. Not my mother. His mother. And there is a void of words to describe her. You know those rumours about her?

But may God protect and keep your father's sister. She was a good person. She told me in secret that she saw your grandmother collecting milk from the goats for you, and when it was in the bucket, she spat in it. Mixed her fluids into the goat milk. And then gave it straight to you. So, you would drink this goat milk spit. She did this because she wanted you to take after her side.

His sister told me about that spitting thing. So, I took your grandmother aside one day when she was milking the goats. I told her that I had spoken to the doctor and he said that only cow milk is good for the baby. I had to buy it off your father's sister, because she was the one that had big milking cows. I paid a lot for that cow milk. And it was an inconvenience. And then when we left the village to come back to Australia, she gave all of the money back.

She was good, your father's sister. But you didn't know you had an aunty until very late, did you? He never ever spoke about her. They haven't spoken for your whole life and I don't know why. I know why. I'll tell you sometime.

Your grandmother's energy poisoned that whole farm. Land and animals. You know about your sister and the rooster? On the farm there were all these chickens. Of course, they had a rooster. Not much to look at, as birds go. Little weedy. Had that hook in his face that all your dad's family have. Every time you and your sister walked past, the rooster would go for her. Run after her, pecking at her feet. She would scream. Help me! Help me! He is pecking me! It was so funny. But you? He wouldn't even touch you. You could walk right up to the hens and play with them, and he would never attack you.

Something else strange about the energy on that farm. Once we lost you. We got so scared. We ran around looking for you. And I was scattered all over the place. Checked under all the beds. In the coop. I even looked in the water tanks and down into the wells. And just as we were about to leave the farm, we saw you in the cattle pen. You were in there with a heifer and her new calf. You know heifers attack around their young? For no good reason too. They just like to attack. We saw you in there and it was something else. We were all too scared to go in and get you. You were in there playing, like the calf was a puppy or something. The cow looking on. We had never seen anything like that before. We had to lure you out with lollies. And your grandmother. Oh, she was pleased with seeing you in there. Her magic ways were working on you. You—the grand boy! Who ended up being gay! Ha!

But there are other things about your father's mother. Things you wouldn't believe. That would open your eyes and make them go—wah! She thought girls were disposable. Once we were coming back from Katouna. We went and saw my parents. And I remember your sister going up to greet her. Big-eyed sweet girl. Hands out for a hug. And your grandmother, well, she just pushed the little one out of the way. Push! Said something like, Move! You thing! You dumb object! And then she reached for you. Called you lollies, sweetness, and honey. She loved boys too much. That's why her own daughter never liked her.

Come here. I'll tell you this. I didn't trust her. I don't know why I'm whispering. I know she came from a bad place though. She was dark. Too dark for that town. Do you understand? No, not skin tone, even though she had that Otto-Turk in her.

You know who her father was? Your great-grandfather? Well, a few generations ago your father's family was prosperous. But you know how wealth diminishes down the generations when people are too proud. Your great-grandfather, well, he didn't inherit that much. But he had a sister. She was kidnapped by pirates. Was never seen again. They must have done some bad deals. And your great-grandfather was sad. He fell in love with one of the dark-skinned farm girls. Betrothed her. It was unheard of at the time. Someone in a position like his to marry some Turkish refugee. Must have been a big pain in the community. Oh, what they must have said in the isle of churches! I know your dad got his grandmother's darkness. Meaning that people teased him. Your father never got over that. Being teased by a whole community of people. He spoke Turkic to his grandmother. His Greek wasn't that good. He loved her. But his mother. Well, her rotten eyes were something else.

When your grandmother was a young woman, she birthed your aunty. And then three girls after that. Three girls that died. Until she had a boy. Your father. And he managed to survive. You ever wonder why three girls died in a row? You ever wonder why your father survived? Think about it.

You know when I said there is no difference between Ancient Greeks and Modern Greeks? That's what I mean. That's why I want you to learn about the Ancients and how they thought because you aren't too far off that.

I'm not sure if you should write that story about your father's mother though. I just wanted to explain to you why I couldn't live with that side of the family. I know what that side of the family does to women. They would have sacrificed any woman for some wind. And my god your sister was smart. I mean all the women that come from our side are brilliant. All their eyes shine.

Your father's eyes used to shine. Before the cataracts started growing around the edges. And his evil deeds washed the beauty of them away. Oh, when he was younger your father was handsome. Dark skin. Colour-changing eyes. I got lost in them because I'm from a family of brown eyes. He said that, after we first met in the bank and had our little date, he went around on his moped and went up to the village to ask about me. That's bullshit. I think that's something he just made up. Says he found out that my father was someone in the forces and that I was from a good family. But that isn't true. I don't think that happened. Sometimes I hear him outside when he is in the garden. He sings that old Greek song, 'There is a married woman that I love, and she has two children.' I don't believe he is singing about me. Must be someone else.

You know there are members of your family that avoid him? I remember the look of shock on your face when you realised he had a sister. What kind of man doesn't speak to his own sister? You remember when you had a big fight with your sister and you wanted to write a letter to her, and I said you better stop, stop writing that letter, because that's the exact kind of thing that your father would do. Why do boys end up like this?

Listen, this is how you should start that book you are going to write about me. Are you writing this down? Let me speak. Shoosh. This is the story of a migrant woman! This is the story of a woman that has suffered so much, more than most will know! Oh, how she suffered and never speaks of it!

See—sounds good. What was that cough? You said you stopped smoking but too much smoking other things. I know you. Do you remember when you were twenty-five? You were living out of home and had that break-up and you wouldn't stop crying. And I would come to that windowless apartment, and I found drugs everywhere. And then you started believing things and seeing things that weren't there. I can't take care of you now. I'm the sick one. You should see how sick I am, no one has ever been as sick as me. My hip is porcelain, both knees metal. My sugar affects my joints. I could go on but don't worry about my pains. How can you? You children have had everything given. Are you hungry? Do you need food? Have you been eating rubbish? Too much McDonald's. Look at you.

This time I put brown rice in the spanakopita. It's to absorb the liquid as it cooks. Did you eat it? You look hungry. Are you hungry? I think I sent you some pieces of spanakopita. Don't worry, I have some here that I can heat up. Don't worry about me, but bending over this fridge. It hurts! Now this is a fridge your sister bought. Why is the freezer on the bottom? It makes ice that comes out of this tap, but is it good? This is frozen but it looks good, look at it. I'll put it in this extra-nice microwave. Your sister's house, eh? Now she's a big lawyer, and won a case in the High Court in Canberra. But look around at the mess. Will the High Court do the vacuuming?

PART 2

1945–1950

LEFKADA
THE PEASANT FAMILY

Midwife Friday was flipping leavened dough off a pan when a neighbour yelled through the shutters. Word had come that Torch Peasant was crowning, her moans had become screams. Immediately she abandoned the stove, leaving it to burn the rest of its wood. She looked back to see the kitchen left in disarray—the container of flour and dark bottle of oil still opened. She put on her smock and gestured to her two young sons to follow. As they passed the threshold of the door, she saw one of the boys step into the house and then come back out holding the talus bones of a goat. Good, she thought, they can play jacks with the two girls.

She moved like a nightingale, inscribing her figure in the paths, running from her home to the bottom of the village. Her legs went too fast and tangled in her skirt, so she reached down and bunched the brown cloth in her hand so she could move unencumbered. She was going to what was known as the old neighbourhood. Midwife Friday emerged from a lane into the square. It was a large open space where they gathered for festivals, now empty. Flanking it was the cafe and the general store. Men who were too old for field work sat around. A song about thieves wailed through the radio, the tinny sound from the speakers competing with the pattering feet of Midwife Friday. The men at the kafenio looked up from their backgammon boards and saw her running with her two sons behind. They yelled after her, taking their fingers off the red and black discs. She interpreted their yells as catcalls and ignored them.

Her foot slid on some mossy steps, and she nearly keeled over, both hands extended out for balance, and the boys grabbed her to make sure she did not fall. She skipped a bit and found her footing again. She arrived at the loquat tree in front of Torch's house, momentarily distracted by the gold fruit. When her gaze hit the house, she realised there was something wrong. Most of the outside wall made from white rocks and mortar had fallen. A crack in the wall grew from the ground up, tearing the house apart, leaving a pile of stones near a closed door and the living space completely exposed. Inside the house, parts of the wooden roof had collapsed next to the fireplace and shattered the grain urns. Rain had come into the house, tiny greens taking root and plants sprouting amongst the weathered and broken furniture. She stopped to think, the house was a reminder of her own unpropitious times, the homes she thought she knew much about, which had their own nature, her first home that had been taken away from her through war, destruction, and exile. Her mind swam to those who had stayed behind.

Perfume of the golden fruit filled her nose, the scent stirring her body to the present. Blessed to break those thoughts, she remembered her task. Looked for help and called out to the neighbourhood. From around the corner came Musk, who was considered the village dullard. She carried a water jug and wore a floral dress which was more appropriate for Sundays and ceremonies. There were oil and chicken blood stains on it, ruining the craftsmanship and quality of the special fabric. Musk clicked her mouth, her throat moving up and down as she gulped. Midwife Friday asked her where the Peasant family lived now. Musk groaned as she put the water jug down at her feet, it involuntarily tipped slightly to the side and water rushed out at the top. Musk mumbled a curse. That muttering drawl was impossible to decipher. Midwife Friday reflected on that accent, specific to this island village and whatever condition she had been born with. Wake up a bit before you start the day! You remember the earthquake! said Musk. A big one. Yes. So big that ceramic tiles fell and stone walls split. She had no time for her own embarrassment. Musk! Now tell me where the family are! Midwife Friday extended her palms out in front of her, she curled her fingers in rolling waves to elicit the knowledge out of the woman. The family had moved to a rental. After all this time, it seemed that their house had not been rebuilt. They were living near the top of the village, just to the right of where the school was.

Three thank yous from Midwife Friday and she pulled up her skirt in folds. She called the two boys to follow. They crisscrossed through the veins and arteries of the village. She blessed the paths that were made up of mortar and stones so smooth that her children could go barefoot without hazard. She blessed this village and everyone that lived there, who broomed their paths and adopted different sections to keep them free of leaves and twigs. It was work but it also kept the community together, and she knew that it served another purpose. While they did their duties for the neighbourhood, they talked amongst themselves and kept abreast of important things to monitor. Like which girl was one of the smart ones and would need extra books, which boy was too handsome and silly, which family would need extra help this winter but were too proud.

Midwife Friday passed the cafe again. One of the oldies yelled out to her. We tried telling you! You Turks are too quick! The men pointed her in the direction of the house. Since the forced migration, running through villages created a single-minded response in her. All other sounds turned off and she focused on the place in front of her and what was needed to get to it. Sound was just a distraction. This focus served her well at times, in the last few years the distant whistle of mortars and the crack of shotguns could be blocked out while her eyes were stuck on a woman who was crowning, listening to the tempo of her breath as it quickened. It was a useful skill for a midwife, pulling out a baby while guns popped across the hills. This power was part of her now, it had helped her escape the predominantly Greek village she had come from in Asia Minor when it had been attacked by Ottomans. It had led her to become one of the many refugees involved in the grand population exchange of the two countries. But other times, such as now, she missed important information. My single focus has helped me, she thought. My sons are safe, in this high mountain village on an island.

Those sons kept on the tail of her dress now. She pumped her legs, approached the top of the village. Around her the houses seemed to look down on the ledge of the mountain. Just past them was a ledge that went all the way to the summit. There was something scary about being too close to the sky, she thought. At least the other houses were protected. The wailing sounded like a gale, but it indicated that Torch Peasant was birthing. She followed the sounds to the right house. Outside, sitting on the steps, were two girls. They were the two heralds of the newborn. Both were holding their knees and rocking back and forth. Midwife Friday kneeled to reassure them—she knew each child and had guided them out too. She knew each child's character. How the elder one needed to be distracted and the younger one was scared only for the eldest, never herself. Before she disappeared into the house, she looked at her sons and pointed to the two girls. The eldest was named Open Sea and the youngest was called Very Foreign.

•

Soon we will have a new baby in the house! said Open Sea. She was talking to the two boys of Midwife Friday. She was excited to get the attention from the older boys, so much more mature than her. These boys had even started going to school! When they had first asked to play, one of the boys—which one, she could not tell the difference—opened his palm and revealed the bone jacks. She ordered them all to form a circle to play and they listened to her as she was the oldest girl.

As they played, Open Sea looked behind her to the windowpanes beaten by the sun. The sounds of wailing came out of the house. She knew that through the walls was the quick beating heart of her mother. So many times, she had placed her ear on the breast of her mother and heard that heartbeat and then put her palm on the stomach to feel the unborn baby. From what she remembered, like the time when the donkey gave birth, she assumed Midwife Friday would be kneeling underneath her mother while her mother stood, waiting for the baby to fall out.

Although her mother's wailing was distracting, she knew village life went on. Up the hill a horse with flat iron hooves walked around in circles over the scythed wheat, milling it into flour. Goats climbed vertical rocks, stood awkward and bleated their tragic songs into the air. Down in the middle of the village, elderly men sat listening to news and music, spitting and hunching. Chickens were stalked by foxes, who hid just out of sight in the forest beyond the village. And in the surrounding mountains, the dark-bearded men, which the adults called guerrillas, wore their stolen army uniforms and kept fighting those foreigners who parachuted down from the clouds.

Open Sea had a bone jack on the back of her palm. She threw it up and turned her hand over to sweep up as many pieces as she could on the ground. She picked up four. Her sister, Very Foreign, asked the boys why Midwife Friday spoke in broken Greek. Was she a foreigner like the army men who came from the sky and sea? One of the brothers had his turn, he snatched up two bone jacks. Their mother spoke in broken Greek because she had learned Greek when she was older, she came from a place called Asia Minor. They did not remember their old tongue. The other boy threw a jack high into the air and picked up two bones and kept chattering away. Their real dad had been killed in wartime. The place they came from was a village in the land of the east. When they asked their mother, she said something about red liquid pouring on the black leaves of the laurel bush.

When the yelling and groans inside the house stopped, Open Sea turned to face the house. The boys kept throwing their pieces into the air, bones of a goat landing on the soft earth. Open Sea stood up, took slow steps towards the front door. The sound of a wailing infant travelled towards her. She shared a glance and nod with her sister, they gave each other permission to go forward. Peering into the crack of the door, she could almost see. Her two palms pressed against the wood to open the door more fully. Her head inside, she saw her father sitting on the low stool. His chest was resting on top of his knees, his face staring down at the ground. He was a still ball. Her mother was alone in the bed, her head rested on its side, beads of perspiration collecting under the ridge of her eyebrow. She could see her mother's long black hair; it shone with sweat and framed her head like the All Holy Mother. It was one of the few times where she was not wearing the traditional brown head covering. Her mother looked away from everyone, her eyelids struggling to stay open. Something was settling underneath her eyes. It looked like she was sad.

Open Sea was drawn to the baby. Midwife Friday swayed the bundle in her arms and looked up to see the two little girls. The room smelled of the innards of a human, exhausted breath rising from all the people. There was a crack of sunlight sneaking through the windowpane. With their mother looking away and their father distant, the girls asked the name of the child. Because of tradition, no one would name the baby until it was baptised. But it was a girl. For a month and a few days, she would be called Beba.

While the adults rested in a sad way, Beba was passed from child to child. Her father kept offering things to Midwife Friday and she refused any payment. Open Sea was told to grab a chicken and put it in the hands of one of the boys. Midwife Friday kept saying no, like she was playing a game. Open Sea was learning the rules of hospitality. The protocol of initially refusing generosity until it was offered with force. One of Midwife Friday's sons was summoned into the house. Open Sea put the red fowl in his arms. The chicken shook its head and surprisingly acquiesced to being squished under the boy's arms. Open Sea still could not tell the brothers apart.

•

Torch Peasant could hear her two daughters chanting the names of their family. She thought it a sweetness and a spell. Mama. Baba. Beba. Open Sea. Very Foreign. The two girls kept repeating the names of the family members. Torch went outside to see them, they were stirring five pebbles on the ground, like a cauldron on the earth. They looked up at her and smiled. She went back to sweeping the living space with a straw broom. She relished that the handle of the broom had been cut exactly for her height, she could hold it low with one hand and its fanned bristles would graze across the floor. In her other arm she held the tightly bound newborn, Beba.

The bristles were soft enough to wipe away the debris that had collected on top of the hand-loomed rug. Torch reminded herself to be extra careful, she had made the rug herself using a pattern she knew, one that belonged to Lefkada herself. Little diamonds in green and gold with arrows shooting across the fabric. It was her own personal luxury, and it chanted its own pride. As the broom went over the rug, she realised that it was too dirty to be left on the floor. There were too many specks of dirt and little leaves.

Because of the new baby, it would not be uncommon for guests to pass through. They might see her messy floor.

Criticism might sweep around the neighbourhood in low tones! The gossip might even end with a neighbour crossing themselves and saying: God would not want a glorious male heir for that house with its dirty rug. She worried about this as tiny particles of dust rose from the ground and clung to her hemline. She decided she would raise it over one of the tree branches outside and beat it down, leave it up so that the mountain breeze could pass through its threads. She would do this while her three children were inside the home. The eldest, Open Sea, would be tasked to keep her eye on the newborn, even though she was only a few years older than the baby. Torch decided to bribe her. If the child did her job, she would be rewarded with a spoonful of cherry jam with a basil leaf on top.

Torch dragged the rug outside; she shifted her weight while throwing the rug over the branch of an Aleppo pine. This was easy compared to holding children all day. She hung it over a lower branch, to reach at all the parts. She pinched and pulled at each corner so that the rug was draped all over the needles of the tree, then her fingers pressed down on the golden and green geometric patterns to break the pine needles underneath and release their scent.

Torch looked up to see three local women coming to visit her. All of them had emerged from the same side path and must have come from the middle neighbourhood. Initially surprised by their visit, she greeted each of them with three customary kisses. In their hands they held gifts. They brought baby garments and a special dish of glossy legumes. Torch received their gifts with gratitude, she thanked them for coming round, apologised about not being ready for guests and then offered to boil them coffee. The most senior of the women suggested they could sit outside on their skirts as the weather was pleasant. Torch called her two daughters outside while she went to make coffee. The three women showered compliments upon them. They stood up straight, made eye contact, smiled and were silent, just as they had been taught to do when greeting members of the community. They all sat down and passed around little Beba. The women cooed at the baby and interrogated the girls.

Torch came outside with the coffee and some dry biscuits. After settling with their coffees, one woman spoke up. She told Torch that they had passed each other on the way to the fields and had got to talking about her problem. She kept silent, linking eyes with all the women. The problem they spoke of was her having three girls and no boys. There was a sentiment amongst them that an affliction had befallen the family. The problem of the three girls was something that needed to be remedied. Torch said she had been having conversations with her husband about this. The women said that it would be read as a curse upon the family. Three girls would be a problem for them in the future. Inside, Torch reflected on the slight shame of their Sunday public appearances at church that were accompanied by glances of pity.

Respectfully, she listened to them. They were all older than her, had married their daughters off to suitable land workers and policemen—one of the daughters had even married a merchant.

Some of their sons were doing military service, another had been killed by Italians and another was a mute and stout workhorse. Never having had a mother herself, Torch listened to the words of the elder women with austere ears. They knew their blessings, their luck in life as women and as elders. She knew their role in guiding new brides in the ways of village life and she had fond memories of their generosity. In the past they had made sure she had ample brown fabric for the skirt, corset and head covering that would be required of her to wear. The colours of a married woman. She had heard of their work in the community. Telling women to pull down their sleeves to make their bruises more discreet while at the same time having a word to the men. Torch accepted this information as a gift.

She yearned for a male child, who wouldn't? When she had been pregnant, she had skirted around her desire, wary of how intentions skewered the delicate harmonies of childbirth. She thought of her own mother, who had died delivering her twin brothers. There were no women available to take care of the newborns so they had been discarded next to their mother's corpse until they died. The unbaptised and nameless twins were disposed of, while their mother got a burial that was a sacrament. Torch had experience as an orphan, and it put a fear in her. She understood the balances of life. She understood how any showy displays could be used against her. A rule they knew, hubris or excessive pride would be repaid tenfold in pain. Torch kept her body decorated with protective amulets. She touched the evil eye on her wrist. She also understood that, if fate had swung differently, she would have been one of those dead twins. That darkness within her led to suspicion of the balance of fleshly wants, which she remedied with prayers to saints, Jesus, and the All Holy Mother.

Sitting out the front of her house, listening to the women's concerns, she realised she wanted a male heir, and this was a sign. God had enunciated through community, and this message allowed her to guide her intentions to affect fate. She knew there was danger in bending the line of His Will. Her origin was a constant caution. But then again, she reasoned, what fate is it to have a stepmother who never even spat in her direction? She was now over thirty years old and still fertile. Her husband was of age and soon might not be able to produce. But what tipped her to guiding fate to try and favour her was something else. It was never said aloud, but it was the way they looked at her. When she passed the other neighbours during her daily tasks such as collecting water, or other times when she walked down the valley to wash her clothes in the stream, there would be the official greeting. Hello and then a pause. And then the women, neighbours or whoever, would tilt slightly to the side in examination. A subtle angle of the head, eyes expanded and mouth closed. Words were not needed. It was in this, the subtlest of gestures, that Torch learned that her worth as a woman would be nothing until she produced a male heir.

•

Spirit could see his hands in the dark, they reached out to the bulbs of garlic, hanging in the airless store. He broke off a segment and swallowed it whole for vigour. The smell of the seeds and grains were in the air. Nutty, metallic, familiar; the mineral rich scent of earth and her children reaching into his nostrils. There was a small barrel underneath the harvesting seeds and bulbs, it was filled with salt and offcuts from the goat they had killed for the Feast of the Resurrection. The next time he had low energy he would ask his wife Torch to cook parts of the liver. Spirit put his hand in the coarse and dirty salt, stirred the crystals, some of them getting caught on the hairs of his knuckles. It was the texture of salt that satisfied, the rough particles against his fingertips, coarse rocks on a beach, reminding him of his past. He took a jar down from the shelf, it was filled with the seeds of pulses. They would grow in any kind of terrain and there was an old rocky field to the side of the main groves where he could plant them. He exited the stores and walked out into the living space. There was wood in the fireplace, some red embers around the ashen blocks. The loomed rug on the floor was dirt free, the tin buckets were clean, there was no dust on any of the ornaments or icons. Torch was what they called a victory wife, a gorgeous homemaker, clean and always spirited. His blue woollen coat hung on the wall; it was his favourite, but he did not don any of the clothes of the gendarmerie—a war was waging around them. To be mistaken for one of the combatants by any of the Germans or Italians would mean death. He took another coat, and pulling the door behind him, he left the house. The sun's rays were creeping over the cliffs.

He walked through the plaza. There was no life yet and the cafe's chairs were stacked up inside, the shopkeeper of the general store still had his door closed. But one of the local boys passed him, his clothes mud-strewn, holding dirty shoes in his hands. Spirit knew the boy called His Virtue. He was not much older than his girls and Spirit already had his eye on him for one of his daughters. His family was guided by a headstrong woman who was considered the matriarch of the guerrilla resistance. They nodded to each other. The boy had a tired face and a large pack on his back. From the look of the boy and time of the day, Spirit assumed he must have been running supplies to some of the fighters. Spirit kept mute, didn't say anything as the boy limped along. Although the boy came from a family that had many sons, there was a preciousness to the child in Spirit's eyes. If he himself had a son, he would never send him on dangerous tasks. A boy! Just a boy! Required to trek through mud and forest and deliver weapons! The shame of his pride ran down his fingertips. If he ever had his own male heir, he would be conflicted in allowing him to fight. To be at service to those more vulnerable. Was the cause of the communists as just as a young boy's risk?

He approached the path that he needed to take to get to his field and then hesitated. Superstition overcame him. Thinking he would pray he made a quick detour to the church. Darting in between houses he arrived at the church and pushed himself into the narthex. A small donation of coin was plated, and he picked up a long candle. He lit the votive and buried it into the grains, pushing it down until it touched the bottom of the box. He could not resist putting his fingers in the sand to feel its texture. As flames lit in front of the icon of the Saint That Should Be Honoured, his stomach gurgled then calmed. He said the prayer of the lord while holding his hand on his heart. As he recited the incantation, he forgave himself for the vain thoughts he had. To give himself grace, he put his three fingers together. Index, forefinger, and thumb. It reminded him of the trinity, and he crossed himself three times, ending the ritual. The room was lit by a fraction of candlelight, creating a glow around him. Bathed in the light, he looked at the outline of the icons and the scent of frankincense stirred him.

The creaking of the door behind him announced the arrival of the priest. Spirit read it as a sign of importance. He turned around to see the man clad in black, holding a bag of sand, closing the door behind him just as a leaf blew in. Priest almost stepped back when he saw Spirit. He corrected this stance, let the bag of sand down and then held out his hand, all the while looking away. Spirit reached out and wrapped the priest's hand in his hand, bowed in a supplicant gesture and kissed his fingers. Bless you, my child, the priest said to him. He asked what Spirit was doing there. It was not a name day of the saints and ceremonial holidays were far off. Spirit said that he was contemplating the unfairness of his experience. Priest put down his bag and asked if his guest would help change the sand in the candle box. He pulled out an empty bag and a scoop and they started the task.

Priest put the empty bag in Spirit's hands, he took the only two lit candles and placed them in a holder, crossed himself three times haphazardly. With the scoop he scraped out the top layer of sand and emptied it into the bag. Spirit talked about his three blessed daughters but how there was a want in him for a son. Someone that he could talk to about his own experiences, the life that he had lived, someone that would carry on his name. The priest sighed. He finished emptying the candle box of its wax-dripped sand. He said to Spirit: A name will never be a legacy under the eyes of the Holy Father. Spirit contemplated what would be done with his fields if he never had a son, would they become overgrown with amaranth and nettles? Who would protect his daughters from gangsters and brigands as he aged? Who would learn to pipe and shoot his muscat? He wondered aloud if this was his vanity talking, if letting his mouth speak to his inner longings was ungracious, especially under God.

Priest put down the scoop and put his hands out, gesturing to Spirit to hand him the new bag of sand. As the bag was passed to him, he told him not to believe the old ways of superstitious curses, that all children were blessed. There was a slight heave from his stomach as he swung the bag up with his arms and tipped it over the box. As the sand came out, each grain flowed on top of each other and expanded out over the sandbox. Priest emptied the bag, shook the last few bits out, then turned back.

There were ways to appeal to higher powers, the already passed saints, All Holy, could intercede on his and his family's behalf. He folded up the bag into squares and put it next to the scoop. Because the saints were already in heaven themselves, they had a closer ear to God, the prayer to God could come through them. His palm was flat and extended outwards to the icon of the island saint. Priest noted that Spirit's latest daughter had not been christened, it would be time to pick a name for little Beba and the choice they made should be a dedication. They could choose a saint that was close to the day she was born and known for conveying living prayers to God. It would be even better if the saint they chose was connected to the land they lived on. The child's dedication to the saint who was protector of the island could help bend the ear of God.

There was also something else he could do, the priest said. This was a holy island, where many monks and hermits had made their home. Their spirits had connected to the cliffs and caves. In all parts of this place, amongst the forests and basins, along the cliffs and rock formations, there were places that had been set up by monks, and a baptism at one of these places might play a pivotal role, amplifying the prayers, in service of this great intercession. Spirit asked if there were any places nearby, and Priest spoke to him about the Cells of the Holy Fathers. It had a long history with the beginnings of Christendom and was founded after the first Ecumenical Council of Nicaea. Three Holy Fathers had left this great Ecumenical Council and travelled across the Aegean Sea, across the landmass of Central Greece onto the island of Lefkada. When they arrived here they roamed the interior of the island and settled in the caves to pray and fast. Although the three men were long dead, some nuns had set up a small order there, to maintain their memory. Spirit asked how far the Cells were, the priest said it would take a few hours by foot through the forest.

•

Spirit took the goatling away from its tribe. It sang out to its group, and they sang back. He dragged the thing, a rope around its neck and it kept on turning its head to chew it away. Spirit reached to cover his own ears, to lessen the noise of its crying, but realised he needed two hands to tow the thing. As the goat songs from its tribe became distant, he fed it stale bread from his pocket to calm it down and for it to follow him. Outside his home, he stood astride the animal, holding it firmly between his knees. He took out a knife from his pocket and dug it straight into the animal's neck, cutting it where it would lose most of its blood.

Its body jutted, legs akimbo, hitting directionless, aiming at air. The shins of his clothes were blood splattered. His hands glistened red. Once the animal went limp, he heaved it up to hang upside down from a tree. Tied it from its legs. More blood poured out of its neck slit and slowly dripped onto the cobblestones.

When the blood had completely spilled onto the earth, Spirit took the carcass to a slope in the ground and placed it belly up. With an incision around the genitals, he tore at the flesh and then peeled back the skin slightly. At the throat of the animal, he pushed his blade deep, and it ran down the neck, past the belly and to its tail, the cut was shallow, so as not to pierce the belly. He ran the knife several inches under the hide, to separate it from the muscles underneath, and also to ensure that the meat would be free of hair. His fingers started from the top, tearing the hide back, peeling it from the meat, all the way down, till the skin hung off the animal like a cape.

With his soaked fingers he grabbed at the goat's neck, trying to break the sternum, but it slipped out of his hands. Flies started to swarm around him, landing around the cuts he had made, landing on his face. He swatted them away, realised the gesture would have no use and called out to his daughters to bring him the gloves. The second one—Very Foreign—responded to his call and came out to help him. She silently handed him the gloves while she examined the carcass. He put them over his red hands and went back to ripping the sternum open. Hands inside the neck of the animal, he reached all the way to the trachea, as close as he could get to the top of the wind-pipe, and pulled it out along with the gullet. He used his knife again and sawed off this part and put it down on the ground. Putting his hands right into the body, he lifted out the small intestines and then the large intestines and handed them directly to his daughter. Go! he said. Wash these at the river and then take them to your mother, she will know what to do with them. He gave her the heart and the liver too, she put them in a sack that turned red with blood and started to drip. He carefully removed the bladder with his hands, making sure the organ did not rip and contaminate the flesh with urine. He rolled the carcass back and forth, to drain the excess blood. The gnats kept circling. He forgot the futility of swatting at them, more and more arriving. He made cuts down the leg, just above its hoof. Slowly, his fingers in between the fibre of muscle and skin, he peeled back the skin. It tore from the flesh, and after going down the side of the animal, and down each leg, he was able to get a whole skin intact. The flesh of the animal was bare, ready for cooking. He wrapped it up tightly in a muslin and put it in the storage room.

•

When the October rains created a haze over the mountains, Spirit knew it was time to take his whole family for the baptism of Beba. His wife had wrapped some foodstuffs in blankets ready to be placed on the donkey. He heard her telling the two little girls to get their winter coats. He smiled as they walked away and imitated their mother getting ready. They tied their braids and wrapped their heads in a scarf. It made him smile, his little girls, showing the seriousness of women. The infant, Beba, was wrapped, cheeks getting red, apple face hidden in folds. He remembered when she had come out of his wife, he was immediately struck by a child born with his round nose. His joy disappeared when he realised that the nose belonged to a girl. A sigh that echoed from her birth till now.

Something swelled in him as he looked over his family, his hands did not know where to rest, uneasy, and he asked himself if it was greedy to be asking for the merciful saint to intercede for a boy.

Beba was to be held by his wife until she was too tired, and then passed on to the family friends that would accompany them. It would be like this all the way to the Cells of the Holy Fathers. There were two family friends that would come along, he could hear them outside the hut, chattering away, waiting for the procession to start. These unmarried cousins were to become helpers for his family when more children were added. There were customs on this island that were conducive to having a large family. One of them was that helpers would be given to a family when there were too many children. Eventually he would have to figure out which field they would be given as tribute. Today these helpers would be respectable witnesses to the baptismal ceremony. Afterwards they would help prepare the celebratory foods. He knew they would be good at cooking up that goat he had killed yesterday. Outside of the window he saw one of the women showing the other one a jar of cherry jam.

Spirit went to the storage hut and came back carrying the goat carcass over his shoulder. He saw Priest had arrived, and the three women and two girls lined up to greet him. He watched his daughters most closely, to see if they had been taught the correct greeting protocols. It pleased him when they waited for the priest to extend his hand. One after the other, they took it with both of their hands and leaned their heads onto it, closing their eyes to kiss it with a holy reverence.

Along with the party of eight people, there were two animals. A horse was saddled for anyone that grew tired of walking. He was an elder steed that had been with the family for a long time. There was also a donkey to carry the gifts and the slaughtered goat they would roast at the monastery. Donkey was a gift from marriage, and he liked her even and calm temperament, rare for her species.

Spirit greeted the priest, kissing him on the hand. He looked over his people and announced that they would be departing. The women and children shifted and readied themselves.

He escorted his caravan of people through the village. As they passed houses, neighbours came out to greet them, they waved, said prayers, wished them well and adored the two little girls dressing like their mother. The community was rejoicing. At the bottom of the village, they arrived at the path that they would take through to the Cells of the Holy Fathers, where Beba would be baptised, this child a tribute to the three hermits who once inhabited the sacred caves, hoping that they would intercede in heaven to grant his family a male heir.

They went through the forest, up paths, and down paths. Cold pins of water fell on the party of eight. Pines and firs created a canopy above their heads that protected them from most of the rain. The women kept the little girls away from the stinging nettle and ivy. During part of the journey, Spirit walked up ahead, to make sure the path had been kept clear. One of the rocks amongst the steps had gathered moss and, as he turned around to warn them of this, he looked at the party of people. He saw his much younger wife holding the nameless baby, the family friends holding the hands of the two little girls. He saw the priest gently touching the sides of the horse. Behind them the donkey followed. His past work at the Hellenic Gendarmerie swirled in his mind. He remembered the solitary time amongst mountains, wearing an anonymous uniform and holding a muscat, walking paths like this. But this path was filled with his people. And he needed to remind himself how the paths had gone from lonely and dangerous, to a place where the journey was a celebration.

When the procession arrived at the Cells of the Holy Fathers, Spirit looked over the monastery. It had washed white walls and he could see which parts of the building had been made first and which parts had been added later. Parts of the walls were built against the mountain, hiding the cave. He wondered about the three men who had come to this place a long time ago and decided that this was to be their camp. This hole was far away from all civilisation, distant from the towns and villages, and he wondered if they had passed through his settlement to get there. His thoughts were interrupted by the doors of the monastery opening. Three Good Women came out and greeted the party. They wore head-to-toe black and when they got closer, he smelled the heady scents of their bodies, they had not bathed.

The ritual of the baptism would be similar in duration to the trip to the monastery. Priest performed the duties, recited the incantations, and a Good Woman who lived there was chosen to be the Godmother of Beba. The child was dressed in a white gown, the same gown that her sisters had worn on their baptism. Throughout the service he heard the coughs of one of the Good Women. She held Beba over the baptism chalice and completely submerged the crying infant into the consecrated water. Afterwards, the baby was anointed with oil as light from candles glistened on her. Under gods and the saints, the child was called Honoured. Her name a dedication to the local saint, his name under a Cross. When it was over, the priest and Spirit cooked the slaughtered goat on a spit. And as the meat roasted over the charcoals, the seven guests ate and drank.

During the merriment, one of the Good Women hid some of the meat to eat the next day. Spirit saw her discreetly parcel it away and said nothing about it, he assumed she did it so that she would not have to forage later. These ones live such hard lives out here, dedicating themselves to God, he justified this indiscretion. But somehow one of the other Good Women found out about this. The meat thief was scolded, and a fight of words broke out after the baptism. His wife tried to talk them down. She asked them not to speak hard lest they brought those energies into the vulnerable celebration and cursed the ritual.

•

One year and a half after the baptism of Honoured, Midwife Friday was summoned to the house again. A neighbour had rapped upon the shutters and yelled into the dwelling that Torch Peasant's moans had become screams. She left her kitchen in the same way, midway through cooking. The oil lids were off and unscrewed, coarse flour dotted the kneading boards. She looked back at her kitchen, it read as an omen that the birth would go as smoothly as the last one. Her voice commanded her sons, they appeared in formation, this time they would be babysitting three children.

She knew what to do in the Peasant family home. Her job was to ease the two parents as much as it was to guide the child out. One of her tools was her presence, she created a calming wave over the family. In the house she announced herself in sombre tones. Greeting the husband slowly, moving her hand on his shoulder to convey her energy into him. She kneeled over the expectant mother and massaged her legs, rubbing her knees in slow steady circles. It was therapeutic and soothing. Using a monotone song, she called the baby out.

It was an easy birth, because this was the mother's fourth time. After the tension and heavy breaths, the family welcomed the baby. A son. With perspiration on her head and her eyelids ready to close, the mother spoke to the ease of the boy's birth. This is why Greeks love boys! They slip out of you! Midwife Friday laughed. Her two sons had come out of her body with much difficulty, and she thought them as heralds that had prepared them for their hard lives ahead. She looked over to see the father, pacing up and down the room. Eventually he sat next to his wife, his eyes becoming deep wells. Happy tears started to fall. Midwife Friday cleaned the baby, she bathed it in a shallow bowl, rubbed its arms with water, cleaning it from the head down. She asked Spirit to bring her another fresh bowl and a can of oil. He did not ask why, just gathered the things and handed them to her. She poured some of the dark green liquid into the bowl and anointed it all over the child's skin. We do this to the boy so that he will have a beautiful complexion. She chanted it aloud, singing it so. The father hopped from foot to foot, she could see his impatience. She dried the baby and folded him in tight linens. Spirit put out his arms to receive the child, his wrists upturned. Midwife Friday admired the fine wave of hair that ran over the blue veins on his arm. She placed the bundle into his arms and assured the man. Every child looks like their father when they are born, there is no doubt that this child, with its round nose and low brow line, is yours. She saw that the child had fine black hairs all along his crown, just like his sisters.

Before she left, she needed to make sure everything was all right with the newborn and that the parents were calm. She saw Torch looking over at her husband, her worn-out face relieved. When Midwife Friday looked at Spirit, she saw his face melting from its fearsome sharpness. Torch's husband was eighteen years older than her. But his eyes had the edges of the sword, from his time serving. His harshness was a requirement of his job and it was reinforced because of it. Midwife Friday knew these kinds of men when they were young, these government-mandated village protectors. When she had first seen his fancy uniform, unused but still hanging on the wall, she knew that this would be a stern and protected house. Gold buttons on the navy blazer, the brown riding boots, these were a talisman for the home.

•

Upon waking the first thing Torch Peasant saw was the compartment built into the wall. Inside it were identical cut-outs of her outfits all stacked on top of each other. Dried shoots of lavender were slipped in amongst her folded clothes. The scent, the neatness of the clothes storage, was a feature she controlled. When the wind raged outside, or the beans were low in stores, the simple pleasure of aligning her clothes, scenting them with shoots, was one of the few subtle luxuries that she had just for herself.

The baby was asleep next to her, she looked over his tiny lids, how small they were, and the little spikes of eyelashes. She ran her thumb under the baby's nose just above his top lip. His mouth moved to intuitively suckle but he stayed asleep. She sat up in bed and took each long oily plait in her hands and intertwined them on the back of her head. From the compartment she pulled out a dark brown mantilla made from crushed cotton. When it rested around her head, the texture would make it look like broken waves in shades of brown. She expanded the headdress into its rectangular shape and then folded it in half like a triangle. On one edge were the tassels and the other a clean line. She flipped it up and over her head, so that the tassels dangled and tickled the arch of her back as she walked.

She crossed herself three times, hoping that, as a married woman, the covering of her hair would prevent the invitation of men into bad actions. There was even a part of her that feared the gaze, male energy cursing her. She put on the matching brown skirt that fell just below her calves and a modest top that was enough to keep a demon from side-glancing too much. The shirt was practical, easy enough to pick up the baby in and carry him down the ladder to the bottom of the house.

Her body was a key to the world, she thought, as she went down the stairs. It soothed her eye the way her clothing was all layers of the same colour brown and how it shone because of the texture. Sometimes she would see the side of her hips draped in the material and admire the fabric falling over her body. She banished the thoughts. Excommunicated them from her mind. She must teach this skill to her girls. The effect of the clothes was to signify role, never bodily adornment. As she expelled thoughts of vanity and decorations, she made herself remember the meaning of the colours she wore. They were worn by married women on this island, and she had earned the colours. And as honour to her dead mother she would don them, since she had been too young to remember her own mother in these colours.

Downstairs she opened the shutters to let the cool air and light in. It coloured the pale faces of the two daughters that were sleeping there. Her second daughter, Very Foreign, must have already left with her father. She watched the two left behind wrestle out of their sleep. The eldest asked if she could boil some water and cocoa and she told her to start the fire.

Her husband favoured Very Foreign over his other daughters. It was too much; the other ones would be left wanting. She watched her eldest get some wood and tried to understand why he favoured the second child. Very Foreign was different from her sisters, as all children were, may God bless and keep them all. She had a natural curiosity that meant she could occupy herself. She kept to herself and was not scared. But she could not help with the digging or pruning. Perhaps he liked to keep her around for company, another body up on those lonely hills. Eventually his son would take her role, but for the moment, he favoured her over the other girls. She hoped that he had not forgotten that the two older girls had a very important task to do today. When the sun was at a certain point in the sky, Very Foreign should be sent home.

She fed the two girls a breakfast of cocoa and water. She instructed the eldest, Open Sea, on which path she would need to take to the Cells of the Holy Fathers. She was told to go through the woods and use her hands on the saplings for stability. The path might be wet and she was to look out for mossy rocks and muddy bits. Once there, Open Sea would be given an old icon and a money tin. The old icon was from Byzantium times, precious, she was told to keep it safe. The icon was the image of the saint of this island. He was protector of this place.

He was the one that Honoured had been named after. He was the one that had interceded and granted them a boy. Open Sea would bring the icon and money tin back to the village and solicit donations from the villagers. This was one of their obligations for having been gifted a boy.

•

Spirit and his third daughter, Honoured, were on a bus to Athens. His mind repeated, my child, my four-year-old, my dedication. His mind replayed the cruel ways he spoke to his daughter when he first noted the bad way she was walking. A few days ago, he had come from the field and his three girls had been playing at the front of the house. On second glance, he noticed that there was something wrong with the way Honoured was walking. It was a slight hop and he yelled at her aloud, in front of the others. Hey! What is wrong with your crook leg? Walk properly! She looked down with a child's shame and corrected her gait. After two days, the leg got worse and her little calf swelled to a size that was too big, so he took her to the main town of the island to see a doctor. She had lain down on the donkey, resting her head by the animal's neck. Her temperature kept rising. When the doctor examined the leg, he said he did not know where the swelling had come from. It was biological. A poison. The doctor tried cutting the leg to let the poison bleed out. But the cut was so deep that she became unconscious, and it was best advised to take her to hospital.

He had always hated this bus trip down. Any long trip. Travelling across the whole of mainland Greece had made him sick of going up and down this country. Ancients said that Greece was where the gods had thrown away all the leftover rocks after the earth was created. Having seen all of Greece and her mountains, and her hills, and her cliffs, and her valleys, and her winding roads—he wondered how the gods themselves could have been so cruel. But this cruelty was filling his life. There seemed to be a poison and even the man-made objects of this world were bleeding this poison. Buses with their black dusty wheels and chrome grills had become objects of embitterment, this one even more so, each bump of the road a reminder to him that the earth herself seemed to be up-ending curses at his life.

Now he was on a daylong bus ride to a children's hospital in Athens. Honoured seemed asleep but was half dead from the sedation, her head rolled in his lap. She was breathing and of the land herself. Limestone white skin that sparkled. Black hair darker than the deepest forest. His insolence, his arrogance, came back to him. A daughter that was so ill that she could not even walk now. His hands with their angered calluses wound into her hair.

The bus they were on was especially chartered and headed straight for the Athenian children's hospital. Its leather seats had no other passengers. When he first got on, knowing it had been chartered just for them, it had seemed decadent, but the favours he had pulled from the mayor and priest would ensure that they would arrive quicker. His old standing had been a benefit, and this was a rush. He saw himself as a protector. He was the only one that could do everything to save her. He looked down at the girl's head in his lap: I must do it all because no one will, and I am sorry for telling you to walk properly.

When they had gone over the bridge to the mainland, at the start of their journey, he dreaded how long it would take. No, it was not the length, he thought, it was the pain he would feel during the daylong trip with her. His insides wrestling with the need to get there in the quickest time and his desire to spend compensatory time for his insolence. His initial dismissal had turned to concern the day after he first noticed the limp. When he told his wife that he needed to take Honoured to the doctor in the main town, she had arced up. She was suspicious of the doctor. It was well known throughout the town and across all the villages that the doctor had predilections for men. Spirit silenced her. He said to her that across all the villages that he had lived and worked in for the last thirty years, each place had a kind of man like this. They were married, they kept homes, some of them looked after their mothers; these men could be found across the land and in this place he just happened to be a doctor. Go then, she said to him. Take the donkey so Honoured will not have to walk too much.

He looked outside the bus window and saw a kite flying alongside them like an escort. It hovered mid-level, looking inside the metal can, and then veered away into the forest. As he patted his daughter's hair, he hoped for her that she would not have to make this journey again. He made a Cross over her and repeated it thrice. When they had gone down from the village to the town, she had initially been excited. She hopped on the donkey immediately, glad for the special attention she was getting from her father. The prospect of the doctor brought out some fear in her eyes, no child would like this, but his daughter seemed excited to go into the town and see the cosmopolitan sights. The dressed-up women. The fishermen. The shop windows with dresses and toys from the city. But her temperature flared on the descent down and she slept on the animal's back.

On the bus the diesel fumes seemed to seep in. Spirit slid the top of the glass to allow fresh air in to invigorate them. Her head stayed on his lap. It shook up and down, turning one way and then the other, independent of consciousness. He was grateful for the sedatives that had taken her out. She had been this way for at least a day. When the doctor had seen her, he said that he would need to operate immediately. Spirit had deferred to his knowledge and afterwards he came in to see her and there were bloody, bloody bandages all around her leg. In shock, seeing his own girl like this and unconscious, it barely went in his ear when the doctor said that she would need to be hospitalised for a whole year to recover. The children's hospital in Athens was where they would institutionalise her. Spirit could feel the shake of the bus. Rubber wheels did not cushion them much against the dirt roads.

●

Spirit left the doctor's office carrying the corpse of his son. The child's body was wrapped in linens, covering him from his head to his tiny feet. He was glad that no part of his son was visible, but people still knew what he carried. From the side of his eyes, he saw townspeople walk by and turn their heads, saw their legs and arms stiffen. All who passed him crossed themselves three times. It must have been his forlorn look, his eyes mostly on the ground, or the gentle way he put the wrapped-up bundle on the back of the donkey. He looked back at the doctor's office before he left. It had only been seven months ago that he had come out of there with his sedated daughter.

There seemed no way for him to look up, to acknowledge any person. Before untying the animal, he went to its head and looked her in the eye. He moved his face close, her iris expanded, her nostrils expelled breath. He breathed onto her nose, patted the side of her face and, in her stillness, he put his forehead just under her eyes. She stood still and their heat transferred between each other. Let us go now, he said, and he untied her from her post and took the path to their village.

Walking together with the donkey, his child on its back, made it seem they were a pair. He kept his eyes on the ground, examining the rocks and mortar that made up the road he was on. Eyes down, he found a piece of bread that had been discarded. It was sinful to discard any food that represented a sacrament, so he bent over to pick it up, brushed the dirt off and kissed it three times. He fed the morsel to his walking companion. He noticed the way she suspiciously smelled it, the ever-careful donkey. After she finished, he patted the side of her coat. People from the main town kept passing him and crossing themselves. Sailors, peasants, women in their dresses, girls in uniforms.

The animal herself had a calmer way about her. She did not move her body when she walked, kept extra steady to keep the body on her back. Exiting Main Town Road, he saw a dress shop and his thoughts went to his daughters, usually he would get them something on one of his trips into town. But they would not want anything now. Buried inside him, formed in his earth, was a deep sense that he had let them down, that he was not able to protect his children. He wondered if they might lose faith in him and all authorities. When he had left with his sick son, who kept vomiting up the contents of his stomach, he thought it would be a quick trip to the doctor's. The doctor would put in a needle with medicine. But it was not to be. He had to watch as nothing remedied his child. The doctor tried many different things. And now he was dead. Now, he was coming home with something unexpected. His daughters had lost their brother. His wife had lost an only son. And he had lost his heir. The thought settled deep into the caves of his mind.

When they were away from the town, the animal moved faster, there were less people around. Spirit kept her on the side of the road. Occasionally mortars exploded in the distance. They echoed across the mountains, bouncing off cliffs. A crack of a shotgun—his mind drifted to murdering the doctor, it could be seen as one of the many civil war casualties, if it were done at night, there would be no questions. But the thought was an indulgence and carried off by a sea breeze. A woman walked past him. She was married, dressed in her browns, her hair covered. There was a copper urn on her head. She tilted her head and he saw the high cheekbones that were like his wife's. His bride. The one he married. The second part of his life. He had also wanted this so much for his heir, dreamt of his own child's relationships, what kind of woman would he have taken? He was old but would have known grandchildren. But now he must see his wife and explain to her what had happened. He must present to her this dead child on the back of an ass.

Was it hubris that had done it? He thought back to all the advice he had taken so he could beget a male heir. The priest had informed him to take this route. The community as well. There was the dedication of his third-born daughter at the Cells of the Holy Fathers. Even going so far as to dedicate her in name to the local saint so he would intercede to God and ask Him to grant them a boy. There was a long trip with a caravan of family so they could pray at the monastery built into the rocks. The two beings of his family that had a connection to this ritual—the boy and his third girl—had been cursed. The energies must have mixed. Only a few months ago, his daughter Honoured had been struck down by an illness and now he would not see her for an entire year while she was interned in a children's hospital. And now, his son, gone.

At a bend in the seaside road, he guided the ass into the forest track. Above him a kite flew over, he looked up to see the bird as it screeched in the air and then planted itself on a branch. They were on the straight part of the trail; it was narrow, and it would go all the way up the mountain. He walked up ahead of the animal; thoughts of his daughters still swirled around his mind. It was his vanity that had caused this. Perhaps he had asked too much from God. Perhaps he had asked too much from the local saints. It was no good to ask for too much. In his vulgarity, unsatisfied with his three healthy females, he had skewed with the natural energies, creating intentions that had been swept up and away, creating a negative pallor on the two who were associated with them. The only thing to rectify it now was to be grateful that he had daughters. Making sure that they would all be educated. That these young girls would be able to read and write, to be no one's fools. That they would be raised and have no predilection for vanity or vulgarity, that their service to God would be humble and at His mercy.

The walk through the forest seemed too quick. So much in his thoughts, he did not have time to just observe, to see if there were any animals around, or to pick out and crush some pine needles in his hand and smell them deep. Just ahead, he saw the trail ending and the village that he called home emerged in front of him. The muted colours of the walls of the houses were a relief. As he took the first steps into the village, he kept his eyes down. But he felt the sensation of eyes hitting the side of his face. They knew he had arrived back, and word was spreading across windows and thresholds. It could have been Musk who ran ahead, he thought he saw her water urn left aside.

When he arrived at the curving path to his home, one step up, donkey following him, he saw the Pine Rugg Tree and his wife and two girls standing under it. Their faces looked over at him, confused. They saw his expression and then they saw what was on the back of the donkey. They understood then. He looked down to the ground and his eyes squinted. All he could see was blurred earth. The tears rolled down his cheeks, he felt them on his jawbone, and they fell on the soil each time he coughed up a sob.

•

Spirit had finished sowing a field of lentils, his index finger dirty from poking each seedling one inch apart in the dirt. It was cold for this time of year, so they would be long to shoot. His precision came from his grief, he knew this. But the emotional pain had turned into work, and it could help him imagine the future, a season when the green shoots would grow a perfect grid across one of the terraces on the mountain.

Something about the dirt here was unique. He had never known lentils to sprout up so solid, all the way to the sky, reaching for the blue. When he had first come to the island, he had learned that the white lime cliffs of its namesake made the dirt extra abundant in a special mineral. This rich soil was special for growing pulses. Talk was that it was so special that international guests had even come to see the lentils grow. Special men in coats, who had translators with them. And the weather had also been wet this sowing season; the harvest would grow well, but late. As he looked down on his dirty hands, he imagined the maintenance required to rid the weeds from this field, lest they steal water and nutrients. He started to rub one finger over the other, black dirt falling onto the earth.

When the sun skimmed the northern mountain peaks, it was time to pick up his girls from school. He dusted off his clothes, put on his cap and jacket. A quick path through the valley and he emerged out of the forest. As he walked towards the school, he realised it was later than expected because all the children were gone and the school mistress was waiting for him. Teacher had her hair tied behind her head. Before his son's death, he thought her a stern ball of an unmarried woman. She had been educated amongst books and libraries at the university in Athens. After her studying, the government had sent her to the island in a program to teach rural students. She kept her political affiliations quiet, he liked this. She believed that everyone deserved a classical education but acted like none were worthy. The things in the world she taught were beautiful objects of text. Spirit was grateful that his daughters would get to understand the poetry of the national anthem and the heart of the Bible and the bravery of *The Odyssey*. Whenever he came early, he would hear her asking the children to repeat words. She never seemed to tire of the rhythm of the words being sung out, first her voice and then the chorus of children. He knew she lived down from the village in a cottage just by the bay. She had made herself a home of books. He had seen much worse

fates for young women and now he would not judge her unmarried ways, he would not even mind if any of his daughters had
her fate.

Spirit took off his cap and dusted himself down again when
he approached Teacher. For his whole life, whenever he had
interacted with any teacher, he would listen closely to see if
their tone of voice would give a glimmer of what the lives of the
educated had been like during the Ancient Lyceum. With each
interaction, he looked behind their eyes, to see bookshelves
expanding up and out. Was there learning by candlelight at
night? This was a reminder of their country's other history,
where children learned their language in secret, in a room after
dark, fearing an Ottoman raid. Like all Greeks, his respect for
teachers came from history.

This time he saw her standing stiff, waiting for him, his two
girls behind her, both facing the wall. From far away, it looked
like the teacher was glowering at him. As he approached, she
spun around and grabbed each girl by the collar, turned them
out to him. Their feet trailed upon gravel and flung pebbles
into the air. After the initial shock of seeing them in the arms
of authority, he looked down, conscious of the dirt stuck under
his fingernails, the shame of his agrarian life. He slipped his
hands into his jacket pockets and strolled over to enquire.

The teacher told him what had happened. His second child,
Very Foreign, was in trouble. She had scripted the lowercase
alpha on her chalkboard incorrectly. Instead of making a circle
and then lifting her chalk to put an upside-down walking stick

next to it, she did not lift her chalk at all off the board. It may sound like nothing, said Teacher, but it was a deliberate provocation. She had been sent outside and told the only way she was going to get lessons was from listening through the window. While outside the classroom, she kept on waving at her older sister through the window, distracting her. The elder girl tried speaking up, and the teacher, having had two girls openly defy her, gave a strong verbal communication to Open Sea and berated the stupidity of the older girl. When she saw Open Sea crying, Very Foreign burst through the door and gave the teacher the back of her hand. All the children in the classroom shuddered and lessons were suspended. The children had been sent home early and the girls held hostage until it was time for their father to come.

Spirit's hands were deep in his pockets, and he felt his nails digging into his palms. In his most measured tone, he told Teacher that they would be punished at home. Especially Very Foreign. He apologised for them and made the girls apologise too. In his shame he turned around and walked away. He yelled for the girls to follow.

As they walked, he spoke to them of shame. His role in authority had meant that he hoped that they would unquestionably follow the rules. Very Foreign said she would never follow orders so blindly, especially if they were hurting her sister. He looked down at his child, speaking up at him. With the quietest voice, in hushed tones because they were in earshot of people around them, he dictated to Very Foreign that she would learn.

He would make her understand his rule, the rules of society, the natural order of God, country, and church that he himself had dedicated his life to. And then if those whisperings of words did not work, he would use the back of his washed palm or belt or whip of a stripped acacia branch. He told her that he was generous enough to not bash her in public.

Very Foreign ran up ahead, turned around and stomped her foot on the ground. She pointed a finger at him. You are not going to touch me; I was right, and I will do it again. Her words were a blow to him. But he was determined. His children would see him as the roots of a forest. He linked eyes with his daughter. She walked off the path and melted into the trees.

He put his top lip over his bottom one, he had to close his mouth tight, to hold onto the laughter that was going to come out of him. Seeing the angry gestures of an adult being enacted by a child, with their delicate limbs attempting gestures years beyond them, made him want to laugh, spill it all open. The brimstone with which she shot her words, like she was mimicking the tone of someone older. He turned away from the eldest and keeled his head forward. Open Sea asked if he was crying, and he said that he was just holding down his anger. He bit down on his lip hard, the laughter trying to erupt from his stomach.

He went through the paths of the village to his home. The house had its windows open, the louvres revealing the interior of the kitchen and hearth inside. His wife held her stomach by the front door and asked why they were so late and where the other one was. He got Open Sea to tell her. Then he instructed his wife to lock up the house. He was determined that Very Foreign would not sneak in unless there was a grovelling apology from her. Torch closed the shutters and bolted the door. Spirit put on a show in front of his eldest daughter, he was more powerful than them, children should sit below him. He was determined that Very Foreign would not enter until an apology was made.

•

It was dark and Very Foreign had not come back from her disappearance; her mother worried while doing her evening duties. For evening meal, they each had a drizzle of olive oil on fire-toasted bread. The bread was served with stewed mountain greens, with just a touch of lemon. It filled them just enough and she saw the food putting a spell on her daughter that made her eyelids fall. But Torch could not rest with only one girl in the house.

When the inside walls became cold to touch and candlelight lit the bones of the house, Torch Peasant slowed down her nightly routine, unsure of what to do. Should she put out the fire or should she let the mica sparks burn? Confused about what to do next, she lit a candle in the room and carried it around. Plumes of breath were coming out of her mouth. The thoughts in her mind on repeat, never allowing a moment's relief. One child dead. One child in hospital. One missing. One in her stomach coming. This one in front of her was the only one here. She must insist on defying her husband's orders and going to find the girl that had not come home. Just before leaving, she put her ear to the ground, to listen to the groans of earth, of where her son was buried, to ask if another one was there. The earth did not reply so she felt assured Very Foreign was still alive.

She looked over to Open Sea, sleeping in the living room. Her husband sat near his child. He was on a low stool and his knees were up. He rested an elbow on his thigh and in this hand he held a cigarette. Pillars of exhaled smoke turned into curls, and the curls waved and wrapped into themselves. There was something in him and she knew to never ask about his time in the gendarmerie, what happened before. Why he had chosen to come all the way to this other place, so far away from his roots, from the lands he had policed. She never once asked what had happened in those places he had come from, where his horses trod on the soil of the Arcadians. Where he had linked so well with people, to the fringes of Macedonia, that he had been asked to become a spiritual father to many of their children. She did not need to ask. The quality of his character had been shown when he called out to everyone after his retirement and wrote letters to people, who would in turn write letters for him, activating a network dotted across Greece. And these letters would find him a bride and a second life.

Torch knew that the years of police work had made him stoic. The only evidence she had of his emotions was when he lost drachmas and they started appearing on the floor. It was his tell. Sometimes she could decipher he had worries, like when the sound of the mortars had landed too close, and then coins would be found everywhere.

As the cigarette smoke exited him, she asked again what had happened with Very Foreign. He told the story. He moved around on the stool. It is a crucial time, he said. We need to enforce upon her the right ways to do things. She pleaded with him, the things that had happened made her this way and she needed consolation, not firmness. Things, she said—the word a euphemism for the death of their boy and one of their girls in hospital for a whole year. She imagined that for a little girl, seeing the tears that her sister shed was too much, after she had to see all their family illnesses and funerals. Torch told this to her husband, trying to make him see her little girl's perspective.

At around midnight, Torch decided to go out and find her daughter. She knocked on all the doors. One of the neighbours told her she had gone to the family house of the young man that she had been arranged to marry when she would be of age. Torch knocked on the house. Very Foreign came to the door and told her mother that she was perfectly fine there. And that she would not be returning home that night. Torch pleaded with her to come home. Very Foreign said she had done nothing wrong and was just defending her sister.

Upon arrival back at her home, Torch started brewing some mountain tea over the stove. Her husband asked her what happened. And she recounted to him what their daughter had told her. She even did the gestures that Very Foreign had done, unknowingly imitating her child doing an impression of her.

She waited for his response. She watched him turn his head like a shadow puppet, he looked over to his sleeping daughter, then back to her pregnant stomach. And then he started to laugh. She assumed there would be a bursting of emotions, his anger peaking and rising. But the laughter was shocking. Ha ha! It was all so funny to him, and she kept asking, What?

When his laughter receded, she waited for his answer. He said to her that out of all his children, Very Foreign would be the one that would not have problems. There was an inhale and she looked at him. Up, down. At that moment Torch saw him again. There were moments in their relationship when she realised who he was, his character. This time she saw that the death of his son had changed him. His girls were no longer something that needed a mandatory protection, and it allowed her to see them differently too. His second child, with all her defiance and pig-headedness, qualities traditionally unfeminine, undervalued in a woman, had ended up his favourite because of her independence.

•

Torch Peasant got out of bed. She pulled the blankets over her husband and the new baby. This was a new baby and she had her health. They would not ask, summon, ritualise or pray for another boy. In the next room, past a wooden plank, she peered in to see the two older sleeping girls. Both covered with loomed blankets. Both the daughters and blankets were her pride.

Each blanket had the traditional geometrical pattern of the island. She had seen them her whole life in the homes of other women, now they were in her own. The blankets' gold thread was on a white background, it shone in her eyes, with repeating arrows and lines that expanded outwards, the design formed into her. Each girl had similar colouring and features, they looked like the middle point of each parent, and in the village, neighbours and strangers squinted, trying to figure out if the girls took from their father or their mother. Their black hair on white faces, their eyelash shine. Their broad foreheads, pleasurably expanding out, of whoever they had taken after.

Five births and one dead child, this echoed as she got dressed and climbed down the ladder. She only wore black now and it seemed like she would forever mourn her son, but she had told herself that once the year of mourning was up, she would change. Priest visited less and less, better, there were only so many coffees she could make in a week. On the bottom level of the house was a hearth and stove, a tin basin that was a sink. She thought of her family upstairs, so lucky, sleeping in close quarters and sharing each other's body heat. Sometimes in winter they all slept together downstairs next to the fire. She was happy about summer coming when they would sleep outside on the landing.

This morning, Torch filled up the stove with olive branches. When the fire was lit, she cut a thick slice of bread for herself and stuck it on a fork next to the embers. She thought the Vienna loaf made from locally milled wheat must be the finest in the world. It was made from the best wheat grown in the best mountain dirt. The mountains were high, close to the sky, and got the best of God's water. Milled under the most obedient horses. And oh! The technique that the bread was made from, perfected by those Italians! Bakers had learned it when the island had been under a century of occupation by the Venetians. Recipe so good it was passed down. Recipe so good that when she was a child, she thought loaves of bread were a currency. Ten drachmas or two bundles of wood for a loaf. Things were worth a loaf or not.

Her wood-fired oven was lit with olive branches and pines— the scent merged with the bread. When the slice was charred, she covered it with dark red wine and oil from their most recent harvest. She was happy to eat standing up and she closed her eyes just as the flavours peaked and ran back along her tongue. A pleasure in her mouth. When finished, she realised it was time to prepare for the return of their daughter Honoured.

It had been just over a year since Torch had seen her third child. Honoured had been sent away to the hospital and Torch feared that she would not come back. These things happened to poor people like them. A child disappeared into institutions and was never returned. She had heard stories from other women. There were children taken by the communists and then sent across borders to become warriors. There were boys taken from hospitals and given to the rich. But her daughter had left at four years old and would come back at five. She thought that a girl was good for this. No high man in authority would steal her for his own child. She wondered what her daughter would make of her old home and how much she remembered. No one had told the little girl that the brother she remembered had died. Torch prayed that she would not ask and decided that, if she did, she would ignore the question. Let the question float up to God. As the bread settled in her, gratefulness washed over her. There was a period where she had listened to the well-meaning women, the elders who had come to her with gifts of garments, persuading her to involve the saints in her vain attempts to gain a boy. Now, she knew not to dip into the same river twice.

Torch walked outside to the squat over the toilet. Afterwards she sniffed herself and used the water bucket and material to cleanse the parts of her that smelled. She slipped the moistened rag under her clothes and looked back upon the stone house, sloping into the mountain. It was surrounded by a forest that was pines and tiered olive groves and citrus. In that forest were red foxes that stole chickens. Big dumb birds called kites that flew overhead. She saw one above her now. Her mind travelled the hidden winding path that snaked up the side of the mountain. It had been made to obfuscate the village. The village was one of the oldest on the island, and way back when it had been decided it would be a settlement, they needed a place that was rich but hidden. She knew her home, as it had been her mother's home and her ancestors before her. She thought about all of this, wanting to welcome back her daughter, to the right place, to the stone house, sloping into the mountain.

Soon the two that went to school would get up and need to wash. They had one day left of water before they would need to visit the taps on the outskirts of the village. She hoped that rain would come and bring its soft water, then no one would need to make the slog with pitchers and a bucket. Everyone preferred the sky water, she assured herself; it was better for clothes and felt nicer on the skin when washing. Torch filled up a copper pot with water from a ceramic pitcher, she stirred cacao into it and watched it over the stove. She stroked her plaits, waist-long, and admired their oily blackness.

She watched the bubbling liquid, the round brown balls of air, breaking the cocoa surface, and heard footsteps coming down the ladder. She turned to see her two daughters, who were already wearing their black school tunics. Standing in front of her, they pulled their socks above their knees and put on their shoes, each buckle barely reaching the hole. It was Open Sea who asked about her sister returning, Torch poured the steaming liquid into two cups and handed them to the girls.

●

On the bus coming home, Honoured sat next to her minder. She saw that the old castle was still at the top of the island, but the large pontoon bridge that connected them to the island seemed to be built anew.

Through the square bus window, Honoured saw her family. The glass was thick and had waves in it, and from a distance, parts of their bodies were distorted. Her sisters' heads were expanded; her parents' bottom halves were made too small. All five members huddled under one of the shelters and her mother extended her palm out in greeting. Honoured looked for her little brother and wondered where he was. She pressed down hard on her legs, trying to rub them into movement. After the other passengers exited, her accompanying nurse lifted and carried her outside. It was a shaky stance; she held on to the hands of the nurse as her leg brace adjusted to her putting her foot on the ground.

Honoured looked around to the town that she remembered. The bus port was her last memory of Lefkada. It still had the wooden shelters around the canteen. She thought she remembered it clearly, her father buying her sweet treats the last time they had left. Or was it her memory tricking her? Her eldest sister, Open Sea, dropped the bottom of her jaw when she saw her. Honoured swore she saw a fly zip in. She was in shock, but Honoured did not know why. Her mind drifted to the sweet treats in the canteen. There might be toffees in there and she shook her leg to get a bearing. Her second sister, Very Foreign, broke from the family and bounded across to her. She was laughing at the sight of her. She wrapped her up in her arms but her hold was too heavy and Honoured was winded. The nurse escort told Very Foreign to be gentle when hugging her little sister. Very Foreign pulled away from Honoured and her face went blank. Honoured could not see the smile on her face anymore, just a tremor of something.

She was happiest to see her mother, who was large with baby again. Her mother tried to crouch but could not because her stomach was too big. Honoured felt multiple kisses on top of her head as her mother apologised for being pregnant again and not being able to bend down. She involuntarily squinted as the sound of her mother's lips squeezing together hit her ears. Her father guided her mother out of the way, he placed his hands on her shoulders. He put one knee on the ground and met her eye line. His eyes looked deep into hers. He brushed her hair with his hand, welcomed her back. Some of the smoke from his hand-rolled cigarette blew into her face. It smelled of dirt, she thought, fires of the woods. She resisted the urge to scrunch up and she smiled at him. All she saw was his face looking at hers, and she threw her arms around him, the back of her hands reaching around his neck, He swayed slightly, almost falling over. She put her head on his shoulder and smelled the earth of the village mixed with smoke. She felt his hand on the back of her head, patting her. A big sigh came out of her. She had a smile, but it seemed no one else did. She asked where her little brother was and her father said they would need a donkey to carry her to the village, because he could not carry her all the way back. He pulled her off him, pushed her back and held her by the shoulders. I need to go to my friend's place in town, I must borrow their donkey! Stay at the canteen with your mother and sisters. The nurse took her mother and father aside to talk to them out of earshot. Her sisters came back into her orbit, hugged her all round and then bent over to poke at the metal parts of her leg.

She knew she could not walk much. A few hobbles and then it was the ground. Her leg was too stiff, the only way she could independently move was to sit her bum on the ground, one leg up in the air, and use her hands to scooch her body forward. This brace would have to stay on her, become part of her for a while. Continuing to irritate. She worried some would see it as a farce. Clanking metal thing drawing too much attention to her.

The nurse was conferring with the two adults. She couldn't hear what they were saying. All their heads bowed together, a church-like reverence, her father glanced up once. They were a bit off to the side, she looked at them. Her sisters came back into her orbit, hugged her all round and then bent over to poke at the metal parts of her leg. Baba pulled out some drachmas from deep in his pockets, and poured them into his wife's hands, each coin dropping into her cupped hands. He came over to Honoured and told her he must borrow a donkey for her ride up to the village. She was a big girl now! And he was too old to carry her! They both laughed at this joke. She could wait with her sisters at the little canteen by the bus stop. They could eat what sweets they had there. She asked if they could go to the sugar patisserie instead. Of course! he said, and reminded her to say farewell to the nurse that had brought her here. As her father left, she turned to her mother. Honoured asked where her little brother was. Her mother said he was staying with someone else. When can I see my brother? Honoured asked. Her sisters stopped and looked at their mother. She told her daughter that they were going to get something sweet.

PART 3

1970

ATHENS
HONOURED PEASANT

Honoured was sitting in the bus as it pulled away from the kerb. She looked outside on the street. Her host, who was named Clear Voiced, was waving her arm, bringing a handkerchief to her eyes. Honoured had to look away, the roar of the diesel engine overwhelming. She focused on the single suitcase next to her. It had a black plastic handle and its casing was a hard brown vinyl shell, just enough room for a travelling wardrobe. Three pairs of pants, one dress, hosiery, and some undergarments. She had left all her flares, ruffle-neck blouses and rayon maxi dresses with her best friend from university. All she needed for Australia was a single suitcase. Her mind anticipated the sweet fantasy of going to a new life. Things would be waiting for her there. She thought about the new kinds of clothes she would buy herself, the different shells, the promise of being a different person that happened after a long journey. Leaving all this behind, the failed dates, the failed university degree, and the failing country. Leaving finally, a breath out; for many reasons but mainly, to satisfy a restlessness. She was getting on in life now, turning twenty-five. Ready to start the next part of her life.

She had heard the radio talk about this other shore, that it was a place of pure gold creeks, the sky so clear that it seemed made of fine crystal curtains. People said it was a long trip, she thought it less dramatic. A little jump. A dream across oceans. She had heard stories of long plane trips on Olympic Airlines. The stewards had disgraceful amounts of cleavage and wore too-tight white blouses, she heard they had too much makeup and dangled cigarettes from their mouths. Her sister said they liked to remind the passengers with contempt that they were not waitresses. A fun thing to see on the way over, these women of curiosity.

The smog in Athens carved into the air. And the marching of army boots upon concrete made the grey palette of the city menacing. And oh, the elderly in this city! They had personalities of brine. She had met them through work, and they repeatedly told her that this city had fallen in the war and never got back up. They pushed her out of the way on public transport. They shoved her in market lines! Those oldies! The engine of the bus spat out more fumes, it thickened the air outside. Her head spun to see the distant outline of her host on the street.

Before leaving today, Honoured had found a church named after Saint Christopher of travellers. In the narthex, she had lit one candle for safe travels, a speedy journey, and called for the saint to intercede. Afterwards, she had walked over the road where a yellow postbox was waiting and mailed a letter to her mother and father back in the village. In the letter, she admitted to her father that she had surrendered to his decision. He was indeed right. It was her own mistake, to not trust her father's decision that was made on a vision he saw in a dream.

It had been said by others that in dreams would begin the journey.

Back in the village, Honoured and her two older sisters had to wait months to find out which land their father would send them to. One day he called Honoured and her sisters, sat them down and told them he had prayed in the church and wandered the fields, wondering which Anglo country to send them to. He told his girls that he knew many people who went to the old Anglo colonies of the United States and Australia, but he couldn't decide. One summer day, after toiling in the fields all morning, he had napped under an olive tree and dreamed that a large bull was swimming in the Ionian Sea. When he came out of his siesta, he felt that the creature in the water was moving towards the landmass of Australia. And so, he would send his first three daughters there when they would be of age.

At first this knowledge didn't assure Honoured. But after the letters from her two elder sisters, encroaching her to jump, to rise out of Athens into the next continent, she had relented. She too had felt the golden air pouring from the continent and it enlivened her mind. And then other reasons came, those heavy ones which called for a quick leap away from Athens and the Hellenic Republic.

In the streets of Athens, all around her rose the grey apartments. It was these new blocks, spreading from the centre to the outer suburbs, that would take up so much of her memories, define her experience of the place. They were concrete boxes with balconies, often with washing hanging from them, which had a decorative effect, reminding her of festive bunting. Most of the people that lived in these places had made their own jump from villages to the city. This Athens was full of people who had come from rural and regional places, only to move somewhere to be boxed. When she looked up at the balconies, she saw clothes made from synthetic fibres with shouty floral patterns that not even the Mediterranean sun could fade. There were hand-loomed doilies hung up with holes that let through smoggy air. She recognised tablecloths, which had patterned thread sewed into them, the handicrafts of villagers. These flags from the villages hung on the concrete boxes midway to the sky.

That morning of the jump, she had woken in her room to a smoky grey Athens. She had started to embody her fears, so when her host called her into the second room, her hands were shaking. Clear Voiced told her to bring a thread and needle and to follow her outside. Her host went into the garden carrying a chair. She set herself on the rocks under an old cypress tree, which gave her shade from the sun. The gnats swarmed around her and her young son played his toy guitar in front of her. Honoured came outside in anticipation of what was going to be said, but Clear Voiced pointed playfully to the needle and thread and said that all she had to do was fix one of her hems. It was, after all, her last day! And where would she ever meet anyone again with such deft hands? Honoured threaded the needle and got on her knees in front of the lady. As she worked, the woman stroked her black hair, which fell all the way down past her shoulders. You washed it today, it gleams like a rock, Clear Voiced said. And it was this gesture that brought the well of tears. Clear Voiced comforted her. It's okay my child—she patted Honoured's hair, fingers going down the black strands—your new life waits. The needle Honoured was looking at started to blur through her tears. She had to stop sewing. There would be no big farewells from her because she hoped there would be more tete-a-tete.

Through the wavy glass of the bus window, the city seemed to be crying for her. She saw two soldiers with square heads, decked out in green, rifles on their backs. They stepped together, both of their feet in unison. Pedestrians parted in front of them, making way for the military. The soldiers reminded her of a suitor and before it tore at her heart, she changed her thoughts. She had grown close to Clear Voiced and her young son. Initially she had feared coming into an unknown family unit, but the husband was an absent sea captain, so this house with a woman and child was nothing unfamiliar. Living with women was okay, she knew that their patterns of sleep and body rhythms would parallel. And she knew when they needed space and when they needed connection. Honoured thought herself gifted at being able to blend with all women, a middle child of five girls. She knew which parts of her were strong and they were when she was putting other women first, younger or older.

Before she had decided to come to Australia, Honoured had wanted to live in Greece and make a life next to her parents. She remembered her high school dreams, wanting to go to Athens and study arithmetic, but deciding on accounting to make a practical life for herself. Her father told her he had many connections and baptismal children strewn all throughout Greece. Anywhere she wanted to go, there would be somewhere to stay. When she said Athens, he said he knew a family from the rural northern town of Greece that had made the switch from the agrarian life. He wrote them a letter and they said they would be happy to host her while she studied in the city.

Outside the bus window she saw family villas peppered between the large apartment blocks. They were usually little houses that had other little houses built on top of them by successive generations. Each new add-on creating a distinctive character to the place. Was this the last time she would see them? She wondered if they would fall out of her memory. The first time Honoured had presented on the steps of Clear Voiced's villa, she had looked up to see boxes on boxes. She had knocked on the door and was greeted by a woman with premature greys and cropped short hair. Entering the house, she did the customary three kisses on each cheek. The plates around Clear Voiced's face shifted into a smile. I can see your father in you! She grabbed Honoured's face with both hands and turned it side to side. Honoured stood still and accepted this encroachment on her body because it was done with a spirit of warmth and familiarity. Her connections to Clear Voiced were historical and confirmed by church ritual, they were governed by something bigger than herself. Inside the house was a young boy to be greeted, Honoured kneeled on the ground to talk to him and he ran away. His mother called him and said, What did we say? He came back, stood up straight, looked her in the eye and said hello. She held back a smile at the child forced to socialise. It was true, a son would always be a reflection on his mother.

The home that Clear Voiced lived in was made up of three rooms closed off by accordion doors. Honoured saw these doors as a change from her familiar village hut. She slept in the room that doubled as the living space. The cot became a seat when she wasn't sleeping there. The fabrics in the home all had florals on them, curtains with large and cheeky roses, blankets with fluffy white and yellow daisies. All the fabrics had the shimmer of the outdoors. She thought of them as a rural family living in the city, their decorations reflecting their longing. The most respected decoration was around the fireplace—a garland of plastic flowers in multiple colours. Some of the petals were made from what looked like a synthetic silk. Clear Voiced had displayed the room proudly. This is the area you will be sleeping in. It was fine. More comfortable than the room she had shared in the mountain dwelling. But the houses here, so recently made, were no match for the village abodes. The air inside had a cold wetness to it. The houses back home were made of mortar and limestone and seemed to breathe with the air. In harmony with the environment around them.

The generosity and warmth of her host reinforced what strangers said about her father. That one of his many unique skills was finding people that were wonderful and bringing them into his world. He acquired them from all areas of Greece, but the nicest were from the northern town of Drama. It must have been the fresh northern air of Greece and the proximity to the Balkanites and Ottomans. They didn't have the shifty darting eyes of their island counterparts. She reasoned it was the abundance of good produce and strong communities.

Something formed in her mind about her father. She had a hard time trying to find what she didn't like about him. It was like every time she thought him bad, she couldn't summon the matching image as proof. He was dutiful and correct. Through the window, she saw another postbox similar to the one she had put the letter to her parents in. It made her long for her parents, to be around them. Her father's strength, her mother who indulged her, the comfort of family. The bus turned down the smallest alley, the long iron shape sweeping in between two buildings. At the corner someone slapped its big metal side, and just before another turn, a young man on a vespa shot by and yelled obscenities at the driver. The driver beeped twice, long, and angry, but the horn of the bus was comical, a squeal in contrast to its grizzled diesel engine. She smiled to herself thinking about this sound. She looked out through the windscreen up front, and saw the young man on the vespa half-turn his body around so he could expand his palm and press it towards the bus driver. Na! The bus driver cursed through his moustache, a cigarette dangling from his lips, and threw his hat down. Honoured looked at the pavement outside the moving vehicle and saw men setting up stalls. They were men from the agrarian outskirts of the mainland. They wore their hats clean and their denim clothes freshly pressed. Even though their clothes were sweet and fresh, their faces were full of cracks. All around them were the Romani, easy to see with their pale skin and dark hair. They had numerous garments on at once, all that clashed and complemented each other. A striped skirt with a floral blouse and tartan jacket. She always expected them to be in any place where large-scale cash was being exchanged. When she had first come to the city, she had never seen anyone so different to herself and her community. She was instantly scared of them. Her fears were now gone and it had turned into a source of pride, being exposed to those different to her.

Another young man on a vespa was now alongside the bus. He was wearing the slimmest suit and tooted his little horn as he drove past a corner of soldiers. They were all standing around, some of them leaning on posts. Guns on their backs, smoking hand-rolled cigarettes. One of the soldiers reminded her of her first suitor.

Her host had insisted that a young pretty girl like her, with the darkest of eyes and blackest of hair, should be courting an eligible suitor. He would have to be picked out by the family. In her cot at night, in the living space, next to the fake flowers around the fireplace, Honoured shed tears thinking that another family she had grown to love was getting rid of her as well.

It came back to her. A familiar feeling of being let go. She didn't
know where it had started or if it would be healed, but the tears
ran. The next morning, she woke for a cup of instant coffee and
walked the boy to school with Clear Voiced. As they dropped
the boy in the playground, she turned to her host and asked
if she was looking to get rid of her. Outside of the playground
gates she was cradled by Clear Voiced, who told her it was her
duty as a host, and out of obligation to her father, that she
should help her find a man so that she could build a Christian
family and further descendants. Honoured felt relieved but the
feeling that she was being rid of persisted.

It had been her first winter there and the man that came to
her had been a soldier. She waited for him in the living room.
She sat, legs together, her hands crossed over knees. When
he stepped into the room behind Clear Voiced, she stood up
to be presented. He wore his dress uniform, and his hair was
hard with a shine. His pants were khaki green, they didn't have
a belt loop but two tabs at the side. It showed off his fitness,
how he was able to wear something that didn't require a belt,
the clothes sticking to the shape of his body, unlike other men
who needed belts or those pulley systems of braces. His shirt
held his body straight and hugged against his flat stomach.
Honoured's eyes immediately widened while she tried to hide
a smile that said nice, nice, genuinely nice. She smiled even
now on the bus, thinking about him. All men looked nice in
uniform. The discipline of good sleep and exercise, of being
a man that followed an ordered path, made a good body and

a healthy mind. She believed it as soon as she learned about it from the Ancients. Clear Voiced introduced him and Honoured repeated his name, Soldier had the same name as her father. They sat down and Clear Voiced left to make coffee. He asked many things about her, but he didn't have much to say about himself. She spoke about her sisters in Australia and how she would be the first person in her family to get a degree. There was silence between them after she stopped talking. She leaned over him to turn on the radio, her hair fell on his lap, and she heard a deep inhale from his nose. The pop song that came on was a Susan Raye song that had tingling guitars. The chorus sang out—LA International Airport—it was a song about loss and moving on. She remembered looking into his eyes. Dark pools of redemption. Both knew he was there at the request of Clear Voiced. He looked at Honoured and she wondered at this first meeting what he liked about her. Was it her clear perfect skin that showed she came from clean mountain air? He could not see her body. It was covered up. She had made sure to cover herself. What did he like about her?

After the coffee that Clear Voiced brought them, they exited the villa. Soldier extended his arm out, offering it to grab. She linked her arms around his bicep and they walked out together. As they turned towards the park, Soldier announced that he understood her father had been part of the gendarmerie. She told him her father had had a long and good career in it, that he had made many family connections, which was why she was staying with Clear Voiced. He asked her if her father had quit the gendarmerie when he met her mother. She said that wasn't the case. Her father was one of the few men who had completed his service and then married when he was forty-five. Soldier said that her father was bound by honour to the Hellenic Republic. Honoured dismissed him. She said her father was bound to get a pension for life. That is mean, Soldier said. He reasoned that her father was the kind of man who was motivated by more than money. And he assured her that she would always be safe once men found out about her father's profession. He conveyed the information in an azure tone. She asked him what he meant. His polished dress shoes started to synchronise with her cork wedges, he had the military habit of making his steps match those of the person he was walking with. She asked him why her father's status conferred this safety upon her. Well, you are protected. Not only does your father have his military connections all throughout Greece, but he must know all the brigands, thieves, nobility, soldiers, and generals. If his character is as well spoken of as Clear Voiced says, then there will be no place that a man who has hurt his daughter can hide. And I am sure if anyone did anything to his daughters, they would face the consequences. As he said it she could feel her face change. It made her realise that there was more to the world than what she saw, that there were invisible structures around her that protected and harmed.

Going past the Monastiraki park now, she gazed out the bus window and she saw all the chestnut vendors standing in front of their carts. Her hands were clasped together on her lap, ready in a prayer position, this gesture a gate to memories. She remembered the night when Soldier had taken her there. Her outfit had been fashionably monochrome, a respectful green. Pants with a high waist and flared, deliberately chosen to show him she was a modern woman. She had also worn them because she was hiding the parts of her leg that had been carved out when she was younger. A test to see if he would accept a woman who had something different about her, a woman that had obscured her fears, to be amongst the modern cities.

The bus engine roared, ruining her thoughts. As they went through the more decrepit neighbourhoods, she was reminded of how scared she had been the first time she was in Athens. This fear had been in her private thoughts, the grind of the city new to her. It was the buses, combined with the trains, the people so close together, all pretending that it wasn't one of Aristophanes' comic plays, that it was normal to be in such proximity together in the agora. Her spirit had a longing for cosmopolitanism, to build a future amongst cities and high towers, with men who smoked and danced, a glowing globe to reach. She had buried her fear of those water-damaged concrete walls and cracked buildings. And when encouraged by her hosts to give the answer of her true experience—she had lied to them. Everything was fine. But after late nights at the university, when she got off the bus, she would flip her keys in between her knuckles to go past the three houses from the stop to Clear Voiced's place. Even though they were houses whose inhabitants she knew. News stories on the radio talked about all of the new Arabs coming into Greece. The Palestinians and Iraqis who were using it as a springboard to Europe. One case was everywhere: a young Greek woman's body had been found near one of the buildings that the families lived in. There was a lack of details, but it spurred her imagination. Her fear was a kind that she had never experienced before, one of strangers and, in a new land, the polis.

She thought back to that time she had been anchored to Soldier's bicep, how he had told her information about her father she had never considered. Some of her fears about the world evaporated. Intuitively, she knew she was encircled by an invisible ring of protection and the main way this protection operated was as a form of consequence to others. If someone did things to her, they would be hunted and feel the blowback. She was feeling something she had not felt for many months. A warm knitted safety. The circle of protection started at her hosts' house, and the patriarch himself, and expanded outwards to the government, to the soldiers she saw on the street. As a child, she had seen the rusted double-barrelled guns in her village hut, the triggers locked. Her father's uniform hung up around the house. Navy military blazer, woollen grey pants—when she was little, she would sneakily put on the coat and find old pennies inside the pockets. Reflecting on these childhood memories with this knowledge gave them new meaning. In Athens, she had stayed with the people he had baptised, a cloak of people, seen and unseen, surrounding her. Men he had met in the armed services (who she didn't know) extended out around her like a hand, the hand becoming a shimmer of air, a barrier. The country was doused with power. The highest levels of the government had the army in control, soldiers rested on the lowliest of street corners. They were part of the shimmer of protection afforded to her. There were the families of the children he had baptised, people he had met as a bachelor in uniform who had seen in him enough character and strength to formalise a bond with him. This ecclesiastical bond had paid off, they were happy with his level of success—that he had blossomed with children, with fields, with a family of his own. Where so many of the old guards had died alone with their backgammon and raki, these families had seen her father's success in his chosen bride. Honoured knew that his children had his grace, it had descended onto her and her sisters. In Athens, on the soil of Greece, she stood amongst a community of infinite people. It had taken a while for her to catch up and understand the layers of this world and how the people were woven into it. That long bus ride to Athens, down seed rows of forest and the dry scrub of Greece, was so far from the village, but she would always be ensconced within the army of her father. And remembering when she had put her hand on that soldier's bicep, most of her fear was gone.

Her knees touched the seat in front of her. It was reassuring to construct an intimacy on public transport. When going towards the unknown, she used the objects in her proximity to have a more immediate and intimate relationship with herself. She was always sandwiched, in the order of things and the things around her. It had started with the hospital beds as a child, and then the leg brace she wore for a year after. Her left shoulder and arm leaned against the metal side of the bus and its window. She felt the vibrations of the wheels and engine through her body and she started to have a relationship to the vehicle, closing in, creating an intimacy. Her handbag sat on her lap, and she lifted her arm from it so she could get her suitcase and put it next to her on the seat. Her knees closed in at the front. On one side of her, the suitcase was right up against her flank. The space had been reconfigured into a tiny box. The bus moved forward, she passed the memories of the soldier on the street. When their feet had moved parallel to each other. And she heard his voice—it said roasted chestnuts—the syllables like wooden bells.

The park they had gone to was in the middle of a bunch of blocks. It was an older Athenian neighbourhood where couples stood around. Some of them came down from their high-rises in the evening to stroll after supper. The men wore double linens and their grey wives had cashmere throws around them. There was a group of young men who had cordoned off a small corner to play soccer. They had a mixed team of teenagers and adults. The leisure space was divided into different sections. On the hardest concrete was some play equipment made of metal that had jagged corners and went too high up in the air. The whole park was filled with the movement of people and scents from the roasters. Soldier asked if she wanted to do a lap of the park before they went to a chestnut vendor.

As they walked in beyond the first gates, a soccer ball flew at Honoured's head. In a deft move, Soldier lifted his left knee as a counterweight and then extended his right leg straight with a pointed toe to kick the ball away. It was as gymnastic as it was elegant, and this movement of his body surprised and aroused her. It left a tiny ball print on his patent shoe. The sweetness of his musk was momentarily released. She looked him up and down, her face blank. It was his scent that she breathed in, it enlivened her, and this created a static inside her. He apologised for putting her in danger. What for? she asked. The boys playing soccer were amazed by his kick, they ran over to ask if he would like to play with them, he indicated to his date. She swelled. Let us go over there, there is a vendor who I frequent, he said.

In the corner of the park an old man sat on a low stool in front of a charcoal brazier. He was wearing a wool cap which matched his beard. His face was bored. He had two beady eyes, his overall appearance was dark and stocky, he was made of chestnuts. The metal circle in front of him had a little sea of round nuts that he turned with coal tongs each time one ruptured. Soldier handed him some drachmas and the chestnut vendor filled a paper cornet. After each scoop of nuts, he threw the cornet up with a slight flick of his wrist so that the nuts would settle. Soldier said that his nuts were the best, that they were not even harvested, he picked them up from the side of the road at the mountain level where they had grown since the Ancients. Then he brought them here to roast and sell. Vendor looked up at Soldier. He heard himself being talked about, and what Honoured saw initially in his face was suspicion. But past his suspicious expression was the accumulated tiredness of years and a refusal to be lured into engagement with customers. She saw in him something she recognised; that the ancient plants and rocks that forged him so patiently, the trees and cliffs that were familiar to him, were lost when he was in the city. His face improvised every time he lost his pastural rhythms. Soldier tried to speak to him of his home, Vendor's eyes flickered, and he offered up the paper cornet to them, his customers. Honoured saw his longing, the man inside was dead. He had once possessed the secret to living, but now there was too much exhaustion, selling the discarded chestnuts that he found from his own village to these city dwellers.

She saw the park as they drove past it. No soccer boys there now. She remembered the crusty old vendor, hoping he was in back in his home, amongst the chestnut-lined village roads. In herself, though, she relished the current absence of the flicker for home. She dismissed any stranger that enquired about her origin and the Ionian island that she came from. No need for anyone who tilted their head in pity when she described her home in the mountains, inferring that she was homesick or provincial. They couldn't read her face right. Honoured thought herself tired, she was in that house in Athens, amongst strangers, going with suitors, waiting for an acceptance that never came.

When she had gone out into the busy streets, going to the sugar patisserie that she worked at on weekends, she saw young men, talking and laughing, kicking balls at her head, unaware of the kinds of ghosts and ideas they would turn into. Soldier was one too—but despite the promise made as she clutched his bicep, he made her realise that her safety here was permanent and in the spectres of people that had come before her, if the sometimes-howling winds which ran through the city brought the Romani and Arabs and all those untoward, it would be no matter. The shimmering barrier of networks would look after her in the city. But would they be there in the next place?

This little journey on the bus was one of many jumps. Her father had been the first one to take her on these grand journeys. She remembered it at four years old, all the way from the Ionian down the mainland straits. Roads were much rockier in 1949. The bus had been enclosed like a foyer with dark wood panelling under windows, seats of leather. 1949. Through a sedated haze, she had looked out the window with a four-year-old's eyes and seen the ornamental forests and then the glass lights of the city. She remembered drifting into dreams, her father's hands in her hair. She remembered rolling up to the hospital after the too-long bus ride, elderly ladies, nurses in powdered uniforms without a wrinkle, their hats so stiff and upright. The nurses pushed her in a wheelchair through the doors and another set of doors until they were in a children's ward. The room was carpeted, wall to wall, and she and her father entered the space like driftwood. There were toys of blocks, and dolls on shelves smiled across at them with rough cheeks. This was the room in which an entire year of her life would be spent. Four to five years old. Her family worrying that the leg infection might come back, and her not knowing if she would see her family again.

From her family she thought about Soldier, something about him was too similar to her father. He had his straight-legged walk, his too-tight shoulders, the discipline of him holding on to the chestnuts and eating them one at a time, while she put multiple in her mouth. It filled her with a familiarity. And it reminded her that she feared being alone again in those wards, in those hospital rooms, doors opening again to reveal toy blocks and smiling dolls. Soldier went away for a while, posted to Preveza, he visited her father, and her father sent a letter approving. When he came back to the barracks of Athens, he called, Clear Voiced answered a few times and said different things—Honoured is busy with study, Honoured is busy with her friends, Honoured is busy with work—until she apologised to him and said that Honoured wouldn't be coming to the phone and that Clear Voiced knew many other girls for him. Honoured was relieved to let this soldier go, it would be one less man in her life.

No. It wouldn't do. It wouldn't do to be reminded of the way her dad had been during that hospital era when she was a child. It wouldn't do to remember that she hadn't seen her family for a whole year. It wouldn't do to be reminded of a time in an institution, wondering if any of them would ever come back.

The bus roared through the neighbourhoods, shopping districts and industrial areas. She remembered all the moods of the city, how its weather could control her confessions.

One night, the city had been empty and the traffic lights hung from their wires, soft rain hitting the helpless pavement, weaving amongst the roofs, capable and gentle. Inside her room, Honoured had been joined by Clear Voiced and her son. Sirens did their wah wah wah outside, their shrieking no match for the rattle in the walls that came from the plumbing, moving water shaking with each flush and shower from the tenants above them. The voices of televisions and radios echoed around, and when the child rested his big head on his mother's lap, Clear Voiced asked in the dullest tone: What was wrong with the soldier? Honoured was not a desperate soul who sought the absent applause of a military man. She recounted the ancient stories where daughters were sacrificed for a cool wind and a woman was left stranded and alone while a husband danced and drank on the island of Calypso. She didn't want to be the daughter sacrificed to the military. She didn't want to be the wife waiting at home. Fear of being ensconced again, in those marble homes, it wasn't the kind of future she wanted. She caught herself speaking too soon. Aware of the husband that Clear Voiced waited for—the mercantile ship captain—she felt she had overspoken and affected their relationship. Her voice rose, and she said fine things about the captain who wasn't present. Honoured was relieved when the owner of the house said that the captain was a hindrance, but at least he had given her a boy and that was final.

Around her the engine of the city was unstoppable, they went past the sweets district that she used to work in. She had found the job through her best friend. Saturdays all day and occasionally on Sundays. When she had been interviewed, the boss had asked about her family and where she had come from. Boss was balding, short, and fat. He was a married man with a face that reminded her of pigs she had seen. His personality seemed a performance, his face was all squeezed skin and sniffles. Unidentifiable liquid seeped out of his nose. Honoured looked at him without any kind of respect, he had the mix of being unaware and confident, which made him hilarious.

The shirt she had to wear when she was at work was a rite of passage. It plunged down beyond her décolletage, showing a line of cleavage she had never exposed before. It was completely tight against her skin, and she knew how young her skin was, she knew the way it flowed over her white cheekbones, down her jawline, under her neck. When she stood behind the counter at work, the line of cleavage would make men stop by to buy sweets for their families. Her earnest and studious—girl at university—personality appealed to the parents that frequented the restaurant. With her chest visible and shirt too tight, she would keep a jumper on when travelling on buses, even on hot days. That shirt made her feel like she was naked under the eye. All the girls in her family had been taught to never value themselves on appearance. It was considered a frivolous vanity. Only men could be beautiful, she thought, but this too had its limits.

She remembered the sugar patisserie fondly. Customers would order while she stood behind a simple wooden counter. She would reach for a paper box to fill with biscuits. There were ones made of almond meal, hard shortbreads that were powdered, and honey-soaked walnut biscuits—her favourite—to be held by tongs oh so delicately, with precision, lest they crumbled. Out the front of the shop, under some awnings, were tables and chairs where she would take coffees to customers. That boss often inspected her work, he looked at her every time she went outside. His office was behind a mirrored glass, it had little slits so he could see who entered the shop. She knew he watched her through the glass. She could feel it.

One day she was readying to close and had brought in some of the chairs. He asked to see her in the office. Here it goes! she thought. She knew he was going to try it. Covering herself in a jacket, she walked in, feeling as if her showing skin might have been seen as an invitation. He enquired about her chaperone, and she told him about Clear Voiced—the dialogue was a long piece of rope to play with. Behind his desk, his elbows rested on a mound of paper, his fingers twirling his wedding band. Why would he draw attention to this now? From his drawer he pulled out some cards with handwritten notes on them. He found the telephone number of the people she was staying with and then called Clear Voiced to speak to her. There was a series of formal introductions and he found out that Clear Voiced came from the area called Drama. Trying to find an affinity with her, he told her he was from Thessaloniki, even made her laugh. He told her he had been taught baking by the Jews who lived in the area. He said he would be sending a gentleman to meet up with Honoured tonight. And they might require a chaperone. Honoured didn't hear what Clear Voiced said, but it had been decided.

What a way to be modern! What a way to live! An employer had called her host, and his words rang out, heralding a potential new life for her! She had not expected this. She thought more sinister things were swirling. The Arcadians were good people, deducted Honoured. They were less sneaky than the islanders and it was why her father's character must have been of such rank, because he was originally from the mainland. When the bus stopped to let on more passengers, she was stuck in her thoughts, almost cursed out loud her own silliness. She shook her head, ashamed of thinking he would do the worst.

It was becoming clear what her life should be. A life of study and work was not enough. She had been told she needed a man to cry her name into the night, she needed someone that could appease the fear of lonely tobacco and raki nights—a fate of unmarried women. To be finally drawn into the world of partners, families, and communities that would become a net and a natural home. She didn't need this reaffirmed but the bus was jeering just to remind her. Wheels turned closer to the airport, there were prophets on the street corners, they wore grey suits looking for the right time to cross over. Even though she had departed the sound of the village church bells, she was still waiting for fate to descend upon her. The men on the street reminded her of the sugar patisserie boss's suitor—they had his too-proud walk, his look-at-me suit.

She recalled the sound of the doorbell at her hosts' home when the suitor had announced his arrival. Honoured had run to open the door, but first she quickly looked through the peephole. His eyes were close together but forgivably so, he wore a cut grey flannel suit and midnight-blue tie. Flowing out of his eyes was a projection of himself, the man he saw himself to be. Anyone could see that he had learned this from outside, from magazines and television, from football and politicians. She believed his vision of himself too! All through that peephole. She opened the door, and his greeting had the ease of semolina custard. Honoured was taken with his blond hair that had grown inches too long. It was tousled with grease and the strands fell over his forehead. His trimmed mutton-chops reached down to his jawline to remind her that there were men who didn't need to keep a soldier's short back and sides, that there were men who could adorn themselves. She told him she didn't have time to change her outfit. He saw her uniform and she knew it would be fine. His eyes became uncontrollable, betraying him, flickering at her neck bones, flickering at her line of cleavage. She decided to go back and change her shirt anyway. Over it she put on one of her fluffiest coats.

She followed him out of the house into empty streets and narrow lanes. They went all the way through the rubble of Athens. The ancient monuments that hung over the decrepit modern blocks reminded her to be stoic. He reached for her hand, and she pulled away. I must make him see how I use these agrarian hands for conversing! She moved her hands around as she talked. They went to a part of the world that seemed made for couples. At first they went to the parlour, and he treated her to ice cream. They sat at a table that had been put out near the park. He smoked cigarettes, she scooped out chocolate gelato and looked up at him. As she excavated the ice cream, looking down at the brown, glistening ball, she asked questions about him, and he volunteered information. He leaned back on his chair and unbuttoned his jacket, the navy tie spilled out and he fondled it before he lit another cigarette. The olive farm that he came from was a business that he had learned from top to bottom. As a child he had learned about yields, about grafting different branches, he took cases to markets and self-pickled his stock. Mainlanders have the best olives, he said. Far superior to the islands. She pushed back and pointed with the tiny metal spoon that she held in between her thumb and index. But oh, our lentils! We have a festival for our lentils! There is talk of it being recognised as a cultural object, internationally! She tried one-upping him. He looked away and sighed.

Over the way, near the pavement, chestnut vendors roasted their little objects, they rotated them, reminding her of a little dance. They yelled out to the crowd, asking them to buy. The smoke made its way to the ice cream shop, where the outdoor linen-covered tables ate up its scent. She sat with her back to the shopfront window, he was facing it, occasionally using it like a mirror, checking the way his hair fell, eyes darting to his reflection and then to her. She thought it lovely to meet a man with vanity. A good pairing might be a man who cared about his looks too much and a woman who cared about her looks too little. She turned around to look through the window of the shop. The interior had framed daisies that filled the walls. Inside were freezers filled with ice cream. She saw adolescents ordering cones, toying with time. Heard greedy children asking for chocolate and vanilla, with old fathers too tired to say no.

His posture was held straight, she could see the way his clothes were tailored, a jacket that rounded over his shoulders. She saw a man that wanted more. He was going to be a cosmopolitan merchant with grandiose ideas and big money. She said to him that she had finished her ice cream and wanted to go somewhere else.

They walked to the next place, she was reluctant to put her arm on his bicep, but happy to listen to his bland talk. There was no colour or smell to his speech. He was speaking like it was automatic, she thought it seemed rehearsed, the mathematics of running an olive farm, selling and distribution, mythos of the oldest trees. Honoured was not involved in these things back in the village, occasionally she had helped with collections. But that was it. She noticed the design of their walk, how their feet did not match up, like the way it had with Soldier. The city became a house for him, and they moved through its rooms. Just in front of them a child clung to its mother's velvet dress as she walked ahead. Honoured tried to carry this image with her and embed it in her mind, it had a significance to her future. She heard fringes of music coming up from some stairs. He asked if she wanted to go down into the basement taverna.

The image of the child disappeared. She was buoyed by the sugar rush. Yes, why not follow him, follow his lead, because his suit fits nice.

They descended the stairs, the music floated up and polluted them. Heady melodies that she anticipated would lead to eros in the air. It wasn't a strange place to initiate a desire, but it was too forward, he might get a kiss on her lips, mouth completely closed, nothing more. At the bottom of the stairs was the taverna where everyone was sitting around tables. On a small stage just above the crowd were three men who wore suits and sunglasses. She wanted to laugh. Oh my! Sunglasses indoors at night! But there was an elder woman, an old Jewess Roza of sorts, who had shiny curls close to her head. She was wearing an outfit that would have been fashionable in the 1950s, a hard skirt and blouse, made of the same fabric. Her grey hair was a nod to the bouffants of her long gone heyday. The host of the club escorted them to the table. Her date ordered whatever mezes were available.

The music played too loud for them to talk. A flagon of retsina arrived, he filled her cup first. A waiter's hand placed pork chops and tomatoes in front of them. Bread sat at the head of the table, in pride of place like it was king. The large and confident woman sang out to all of them, her voice nasal, some reading it as a whine. It was the style of the old-fashioned singing. Honoured had heard it mostly come out of tinny speakers, back in the village. She preferred songs from the United States, they were modern like she was.

They ate their food and the retsina did its job. Lyrics from the older singer were about how a lover's eyes could build a life with a glance, and with that same glance, how easy it was for a lover's eyes to rip open the world. She was filled when she looked into his eyes. The red in her cup was halfway and her date poured her more wine. Their food was finished and the Sousta played, meaning the night was ending. Four men and the older woman got up for the frenzied dance. Honoured and her date watched them as their bodies moved up and down. It was five of them going around in the smallest space, music and bodies speeding up. Then the woman and the two older men careened and flung off from the lively circle until it was just the two men, battling all out with each other. It was a dance, but they were trying to hurt each other by showing off. Crouching and turning, their arms extending out, hands in balls swinging through the air. The baseline of the klarino went oh so deep that it rumbled in her stomach, and Honoured was the first to stand up and clap the two dancers. The rest of the crowd followed.

She couldn't remember the timeline of that night. At some point the music had gone from the blues to songs of sadness to more ancestral pastorals. She intuited them. Those old songs working inside. Even though they were in the city, even though they were in these strange concrete lands, where old marble was excavated and combined with mortar, those pastoral songs still reached inside, and they moved something she had tried to ignore. For all her time here, she had been in an unknown city. And when the two men had danced in front of her, the song of finishing time and death reminded them of a home they should go to. To go home. To go to a little hut, lit up with candles, until they covered themselves with hand-loomed covers, and outside were other little huts, making up a neighbourhood, making up a village, surrounded by a forest where wolves and foxes hovered.

He sorted payment; she didn't even reach for her purse. She took her jacket and they crawled up the stairs from the taverna. The streets were refreshed, the night air was clear, there were parents and couples. Klarino sounds from music somewhere whistled past her, resonating in people's conversations. Her hand went to her cheeks, she felt the heat from the retsina on her palm. She had never seen anyone as indulgent for life as the Athenians. Look at them! They walked to a square with a fountain, so useless and deserted. All for leisure. Was this a life for them? Fun night walks and avoiding daytime responsibilities? She would walk in whichever direction he would take her. He said he hadn't expected her to pay but found it unfeminine that she didn't carry a handbag, only a purse in her jacket pocket.

She looked over at her date as they moved through the people in the square. She was small and vulnerable and complained about this Athens. It emptied her, but she needed to breathe in more of it. He took her hand, kissing the back of her palm. She turned away and pulled her hand from him. There were some large neighbourhood dogs watching them. Athenian dogs loved to look. They sat on their back legs, happy to be taking in the drunkenness of it all. These dogs wore their fur like uniforms, they seemed bored with them and moved away over the pavement with silent steps. Her date reached over to embrace her with his arm. The street spoke, so their voices were unheard, and their bodies empty of God. Her desperation was present. Oh, how she wanted his love and future! There was a deep tear in the night. She looked up to see the moon and heard a gaida in the distance. She stood still and shut her eyes. In her imagination was the blue rain over the sleeping hills of Katouna and, far away, the sounds of Ionian waves breaking over the dead pebbles.

They walked away from the fountain down some stairs, there was an echo of a foreign laugh. She was surprised it was her laugh. She spun around, looking up at the sky. Something came out of the stillness, it wasn't even the middle of summer yet, but the tiniest tree had been planted in her. The pavement, the concrete steps and the hollowness of the place listened, the whole square was listening. She coughed into her open jacket; her body heaved. And they found themselves in front of the Presidential Guard and just beyond him the Tomb of the Unknown Soldier.

Daytime Athens broke her thoughts of that night with the grey-suited suitor. The cars outside beeped. The bus driver guided the machine through the city to escape towards the airport, more stops, more passengers got on. She would be free of them soon and she wondered if Australia would be like Greece, would she need to protect herself from the groping hands of men on public transport? They passed the square where the Unknown Soldier was. The guards were in their box. The shadowy world of that busy night came back. In her memory she had stood amongst the tourists, late-night people and the street dogs. In her mind she had stood near the Presidential Guard, but it was dark, and she was too close to the Tomb of the Unknown Soldier. Recollections of uniforms shuddered through her. A suit appeared. Epaulets floated in darkness. A mandarin collar on a canvas jacket. And there was that suitor, the one who wore his business attire and messy chopped hair, scraggly mutton-chops that her own father would have cleaved off. Her father. Oh, what a man! Merciless to anyone he thought carried the symbols of resistance, but merciful to those who needed care.

She realised that her father was a fully formed man. Compassionate to his loves. Constantly pushing the boundaries for women. Get educated! Be independent! Get competent! Refrains from a time when it was neither acceptable nor conventional for a woman to do so. She was one out of his five daughters, and he insisted they all get educated. Her legs had moon craters in them, she would be no good in the fields. Carved-out legs that made her suitable for education. Even when she was in Athens her father's spirit still hung about her, he was part of the mortar that held the rocks together, his stone hands around her unseen, around the vast sculptures and ritualised bodies of soldiers.

The definitive moment for her had come in that square. She knew she liked him. Couldn't place his mind, even though he had kissed the back of her hand. She walked over to a bench on the other side of the square. There were no people there and he followed her, she patted the bench, he fell on it next to her. After they both sat in silence for a while, a feeling of constriction started at her clavicle bones and went down her body, settling just above her hipbone. Before we go further, I need to show you something, Honoured said. His face turned to the side, she saw a slight angle in his chin, there was no part she didn't fancy. She raised her left leg up on the bench, bending her knees, and unstrapped the binding of her shoe that connected to the cork wedge below. The shoe fell onto the pavement. She folded the material of her pants up and exposed her leg, all from her ankle to her knee.

The calf muscle was completely hollowed out. It seemed like it was punctured in different parts. Where the muscle descended, there was a skin graft that was moulded over bone. Waves of skin swelled and shrunk.

She scanned his face for a response. His eyes contoured and she saw his lips freeze. There was a pause that went on for a long time. It happened when I was a child, she said. It doesn't hurt, it's only cosmetic, and it is the reason I don't wear skirts. When he stuttered, not knowing what to say, she looked down at her leg. It was a deformity and a rupture and when she looked up at his eyes, she saw his horror, and the outline of his face became lost to her, unrecognisable. The magic that she had for those amazing parts of his body, his bright hair, his eyes, and the dream fabric that engulfed him, evaporated. She knew after seeing her leg, he would not ring the doorbell at Clear Voiced's house again, he would not stand waiting behind a front door. He would suddenly be busy. Remarkably busy with his business and it would not be spoken of again at the sugar patisserie and her co-workers would know not to ask about him a second time. Her hands rolled the cuff of her trouser leg down and there was nothing else.

Was she wrong to have shown him? Or had he been wrong for not accepting her? She had been blinded by the kind of person her father was, assuming all men were like him. Suitor receded from her mind, and when the last of his navy tie and grey suit became a wave, she was filled with a rush. Stop acting! Find your own love! Find a man! Have a home and raise your own strange little babies! she ordered herself.

Outside she saw people sprouting around Syntagma Square. There it was. The last time she would ever see Greece in this way. This chaos needs to be gone, she thought. It was all too much and needed to be left behind. This final hop and this would be the memory that would be left. There were things happening, the whole country was stirring with the colour of uniforms. She could see groups of Reds gathering all together in the corner. Some of the black shirts swirled all around the street. A mess of crowd, men holding red flags over their shoulders, standing in formation around the Tomb of the Unknown Soldier. Placards had painted scrawl, and the men wore their most effective outfits. Behind them were families and children shouting words they didn't understand, but one day would, and then came the students— rainbow-coloured, loose, smelly—holding mock theatre puppets in giant pantomime, and the young men with guitars.

She was going out of the city. There were fewer buildings around her, and the bus driver brought another cigarette to his mouth. The roads had less and less vehicles on them, she could see the fields. She could see the sky. The air clean, she stuck her face out of the small square window. She could smell again, and scent memories came to her. They were of the places she had been. Memories of the Lefkada and Katouna, the land she would be leaving forever. She remembered the smell of blood from her childhood. The mossy stones of the forest path. The cherry jam in a dark room. The myrrh and the beeswax candle flame. The sweetness of pine needles on a loomed rug.

PART 4

1989

BELMORE
HONOURED CITIZEN

She woke up and looked at the floor, it was where her husband would have been sleeping. In the space was a pleather mat that he had made himself to sleep on, its texture was shiny and brown and reminded her of something filled with oil. He was always muttering something about his lower back. Seemed like all men had those lower back problems and the only cure was to sleep away from their partner. She knew today was going to be a day of exhaustion, so her thoughts only briefly rested upon his absence. Back in the village, where he was now, they would be getting ready for the celebrations and remembrance. There were times as a child when she too had commemorated this day in remembrance. Through her mind, memories strobed of marching in formation, wearing the blue and white and waving the flags. She blessed herself for the day and said some words punctuated by the gestures of the Cross, hoping the ritual would send her hope into the sky. She uncovered her legs and put both feet on the floor.

Walking past the son's bedroom, she looked in to see him still asleep under his bright covers. He was sleeping on his side; his skin was the perfect colour for a Mediterranean boy. He is a good boy, but only when he sleeps—was a refrain her husband often spoke. One of those clichés, a catchphrase. Despite all those sayings that filled her head, that boy was just what she wanted in a son. He looked like both her and her husband. Had the right mix of their beauty (it pained her to admit that her husband had features that were pleasant) and he would be feted because he was masculine. His potential would not be destroyed, like her brother's had been. She held on to the briefest memories of God's Grace, and she forgave herself for having the—hidden in a mountain forest—memory of her brother, who himself was younger than she was. Broken into her earth was the knowledge that she had been robbed of his presence because of her yearlong hospitalisation as a child. Perhaps that was why God had remembered her when she had tricked her husband into conceiving a second child. Perhaps that was why God had granted her a son. This boy she had was in sorts a correction, perhaps the curse had been lifted.

The green and gold doona that the boy was sleeping under commemorated the 1983 Australian win of the America's Cup. They had bought the cover at Big W Campsie just after the Prime Minister had forced them all to take the day off work. When green and gold had been everywhere for the bicentenary, something had stirred in her son, his connection to the bright colours enlivened him and a new part of his personality opened. This child loved colours; bright things were amplified in his small world. He started painting his toys red and green and used these bright toys as an excuse to live in his head. As she watched him sleep, she remembered all the times she had peeked inside his room. She had seen him holding the He-Man in his hands, making it walk across the bed and climb the pillow to attack a plastic multi-headed Hydra perched upon a robot car. This boy inhabited his imagination too much, just like his father. She would catch them both having conversations with themselves and would yell at them to stop. Was this the trait of all men, to wonder, to imagine, to live in their heads more so than being connected to the people around them? How did they live like this? Her hand stroked the doorframe of his bedroom.

She went into her daughter's bedroom. Points of light came through the curtains, the lamp next to the bed was still on and the good people at Ikea had kept their promise to make an affordable but lasting product. She went over and put a fingertip on it, but it was too hot for touch. She looked over at her daughter, Resurrection was still sleeping, the yellow light hitting the side of her face. This child must have had the light on all throughout the night. On the bedside table was a closed book, with reading glasses inside. She picked it up and on the cover was a black-and-white picture, a girl with the deepest eyes. The diary of Anne Frank. She knew what the book was about, and she wondered why a little girl like her daughter was so hungry for tragedies.

What made this thirteen-year-old girl not have the playfulness of other children?

Her mind climbed into the grottos of her own past and searched for memories of playfulness. It seemed there were none. Of course, there were games and dolls, but they had seemed like training. The lessons that her mother had given her were a form of state craft for family. One thing she had learned was that children were made beautiful to look at and to help. They were of the family, for the family, especially in front of the community. From her own childhood, she had learned this as she and her sisters broomed rugs while their mother prepared stew. Childhood? Ha! What was that? When she watched TV here, in between the news, she saw the advertisements and how the children hugged Glo Worms and Cabbage Patch Kids. She saw girls who wore pink and waved their fair hair like flags. Her daughter had the palest skin and the bluest eyes, she looked like a picture-perfect little girl, but for some reason never acted it. She could have been one of them but had inherited a lack of vanity. She saw it every time her daughter scrunched her nose and pushed up her wire-rim glasses with one finger. Her hair was always in a half-pony with flyaways everywhere. She wasn't going to tell her to dress or pose a certain way. She didn't want her to be like those other girls, the ones that had too-big hair, the ones with eye makeup at church, the ones with eye makeup at the public pools. Going to the supermarket with eye makeup? That showed a preoccupation with one's appearance that wouldn't do.

Why would a mother raise a daughter like that? What pleasure was there to be proud of a dullard!

The closet in her daughter's room was ajar and Honoured wanted to check that she was keeping everything clean. She rationalised that it was about cleanliness, but mostly it was a curiosity, a need to know if she needed to correct anything. She pushed it open to look inside, she saw her daughter's clothes lined up, in order of colour, in order of size, all on wire hangers. It all looked so neat. That pride in taking care of her things reminded her of the way her husband lined up his clothes. His Fletcher Jones suits were still in the suit bags! Who kept all the suit bags? And all those garments! A person needed only some garments, not three distinct kinds of blue jackets. To want more was to be spoiled. It was a vanity. She looked back at her daughter, lying there asleep. Was this what was happening? Had her daughter inherited the same features? Those change-with-the-weather eyes. But thank God not that dark Arab skin bequeathed by the Ottomans. A mirage of her daughter poring over arithmetic equations, the same look her husband held when he was doing precise leatherwork in his garage. Tenacity and stubbornness, eyes that looked for the smallest of stiches or the tiniest of integers. Characteristics helpful in work, but difficult in personal relations.

Looking into the closet opened up memories for her. During the courtship with her husband, there had been moments when she was witness to his true character, but she had been too wrapped up in her own needs. At the initial meeting in Lefkada, he had taken her to one of the cafes in the plaza. The sun was setting, and coffee would keep her up, but she had gone ahead and ordered a cappuccino, craving the foam and caffeine hit. Those baristas had fluffed up the milk till it was an indulgence. At the time she had stuffed down her feelings and thought staying up all night would be worth it. Wasn't it? At the time she thought she had met a man who was a saviour from her life. She had thought herself too old, in a place where love would not strike, but still anxious for marriage and children—which was the natural and right thing to do—and just in time, she had got a chance with this man who had an eye for garments. So she got the coffee, and he had a cognac. He said it was because his aunt had died thirty-eight days ago and he had to ritualise his grief. Now, peering through a child's closet, she wondered if she should have seen that transgression as a mirror to his character. A cognac instead of a coffee? No, she should have been aware of her and his desperation. Oh, their matching needs.

She went over to open the blinds. Her girl would need to wake soon, but because she would be busy with the day's preparation, she would let the sun do it. There was a stubborn streak in her daughter that she wanted to extinguish. It came out every time she tried to wake her child. Under her eyelids were the same colours as her father and she hoped that the fates had not implanted within her the same character. She needed to make sure that her daughter was aligned to her. It would be too much to have a second pair of those eyes looking at her with that wild cruelty.

Giving the sun a job to do would be fine. She leaned over her daughter's desk to pull on the cord, and as she looked down she had a bird's-eye view of the table. It was an old public servant bureaucrat's table, her husband had got it from the railways. It was made of industrial wood and iron. Almost impossible to move. He had brought it home on a ute that had the state rail insignia on the doors. It took a while as he worked on it, sanding and lacquering the wood, moving it amongst his garages, waiting for it to dry and rest. My god, she thought, the man had two garages and a workshop. He had three spaces and she had nowhere to keep her Tupperware, no place she could keep all those pots she did not use but would someday. At least they were pickling olives together, those plastic barrels up on the mounted shelves of the garage, while underneath he had his wood projects, like sanding and colouring and varnishing these office tables for her son and daughter.

Those tables took up too much space, being so large and cumbersome. And they needed two people to move them—both of which needed to be male. Getting them from the workshop garage inside the house meant they needed to call for help, so they tried getting the Korean Salvationists from next door. But when she knocked on the door, she realised she had never seen the husband before. Oh sure, she had seen the wife many times. She recognised a solid woman such as herself. And assumed that the husband would be one of those larger Koreans. For some reason she had conceptualised that the Koreans were to Asia what the Northerners were to Europe. Stoic in culture, stilted in their practices, and in body shape strong and towering. That was what she had thought. On the day they needed help to move the tables, she had rapped on their door and took a breath of shock when the husband came and there was a bruised fruit of a man. Those Salvationists with their military-inspired garb and pretentious uniforms, whose intention was to represent piety and repress emotions. In civilian clothing she could truly see the Salvationist man, parts of him weak and wrecked. At least broken Greek men were dangerous, she mused, it had something to do with the way they worshipped their God, with colour and fragrance and hymns that rumbled the stomach, representing the way the emotions came out. The Salvationists' odd and restrained religion was in vast contrast to the scents and songs that she had grown up around. The Greek Orthodox Church was of the earth and the deities they believed in came from a connection to the land. Along with the rituals of the dirt, of the winds and moon calendar, all of the cultural practices seemed natural to their slice of the island. These people? Who knew what they believed in and if they even remembered their rural lands. She had seen their main church at the top of Burwood Road in Belmore, the one next to the tofu place and—oh my god—it did not look like any church that she knew. It looked like a modern army barracks. A place where soldiers convened. Of course that was why it was called the Salvation Army. And because of that darned and wonderful Venetian occupation, the churches on her island were different and did not look like Hagia Sofia. So she was used to all the unusual ways that a church could look, but a military fort was not one. Recalling the monasteries that looked like mansions or the ones built into caves—now those were religious places! Some of them had simple architecture that curved upwards to God, made with ornate carvings, like the places of She Who Will Annunciate. And then there were other places like the Cells of the Holy Fathers, a place founded by wild monastic men. She understood these monasteries as places where the dedication of spirituality occurred more than the churches themselves.

God and all those beliefs were formed in her spleen. She sensed and felt the ambiguity of spiritual energies, amongst others. It was the reason she put a clove of garlic in her son's pockets when he looked extra nice. Or why every new year she had the priest come in and shift the energies of the house. When her children were sick and the doctor did not know what was wrong, she would summon one of the eyeshadowed women who decorated themselves with silver and gold metals to lift curses with songs and oils. She knew the church was a vassal of sorts, the building channeled to the people, there were unexplainable words for the congregation or the building. But she knew that the men with the black medieval robes and long grey beards did not believe in God the way she did. God did not belong to anyone, God was not owned by anyone, God was not property, she thought that idea anachronistic. Like the pants thing. Women not being allowed to wear pants to church seemed odd. Why would God or any of the other saints or deities care about pants? It was hard for her to wear skirts. The best way to cover her hollowed leg was to wear pants. But because the All Saints Greek Orthodox Church of Belmore had made some edict that it was inappropriate for women to wear pants, she had to put on a fake cover around her leg and then opaque stockings. This was part of that edict of man that she saw as arbitrary and cruel in a way that was unique of men. In a way that had made her give her son an ambiguous answer when he asked if God existed. She wanted to say she would believe in the ways of women, in their pagan amulets, in their rules of no whistling indoors, the precious nature of bat bones and the ability to identify moon cycles. This is why I do not believe that word of man claiming to speak for God, she thought. She looked down at her daughter, sleeping next to the book of Anne Frank. When this one would grow up and become a teacher like her, then she too could tutor children against the words of men.

She peeped outside the blinds at the garden they had planted. There was a massive net covering the fig tree, its goal to protect the ornaments from the flying marsupial thieves. Their grapevines had been tumultuous that year, fruit spouting like cheap baubles. The leaves were fuzzy and dark green, so rich, so perfect for wrapping homemade rice stuffing. The garden was bearing under the antipodean sun and if left unattended, it would grow uncontrollably or become ravished by outside forces.

The richness of the garden reminded her of her husband, of the man she had taken to marry. She looked at her sleeping daughter again and wanted to wake her to tell her about her future. She wanted to tell her what she would be and what kind of man would be suitable for her. She wanted her daughter to be with a man who supported her studies and education, a Greek man who was tall, tall enough to breed some height into the family but also retain their Greek features, their Southern European characteristics. She wanted her daughter to take a man that was pliable, susceptible to her will so he could be moulded. Without warning, the feeling of wanting a cigarette filled her, she felt it down her arms, she felt it in her fingers that jumped at the tip. She needed a cigarette.

Leaving her daughter's room, she went to the bathroom. She ran the faucet to get the coldest water and scooped it into her palms and onto her face. As the water hissed, she took a breath. The bathroom was themed blue and meant to be calming, but minute details ruptured her. The ceramic blue tiles on the wall were surrounded by an uneven grout that fit them together. The divider between the shower and the bathtub was made of a transparent plastic and inside it were fake fish and a real net cast over some seashells. The fish looked ready to be startled and swim away but were frozen in the plastic. It reminded her of the sea, of the men in her life, in-laws and such who had spent their childhood casting nets over the ocean, living and sleeping on boats. Once the sea had been labour, it had been work, a task on a list. And here, in this new land, this work had become a decoration. They had replaced the expanse of fields and seas with factories, the boats and water part of that romantic past, a transformed thought. In the good rooms of relatives, she had seen cross-stitches of shepherds on mountains in gilded frames.

Hardships were now a frou-frou. Is this what it meant to be in a foreign land that was far, far away? Their past lives on the seas and fields were to be what? Another decoration?

The sound of the faucet running was a rhythm and her husband's blue tin of Nivea sat on the shelf. She noticed how clean the tin was, meticulous. Fresh as the day it had been purchased. No greasy fingerprints on it, like there were on her bottle of Oil of Ulan with its little clumps of white cream on the side of the lid. A while back, after she had squeezed the last bits of moisturiser from her black and pink bottle, she had decided to use some of his. She had scooped the white right out of the middle, rubbed it on her skin and noticed the texture was like a solid oil. Although it felt like an industrial product, she understood its appeal to him. She must have left a large fingerprint behind because he asked her if she had used it, holding up one eyebrow suspiciously. She said yes and he said nothing. Now she scooped both hands under the running water again and created a pool in her palms, she bent over to splash her face and the water went right into her open eyes, irritating under her eyelids. She felt the sting and cold bits of water went in her nose and she was alert. She reached for the towel and pressed the plush against her face.

The way she washed and ironed those towels was her own personal luxury. It was part of the trivial things that gave her a sense of the grand because she did not have money to spare. When the clock turned ever so slowly and the space between hands needed to be filled, she attended to those towels. She had time that needed to become something and so to distract herself she would iron. The lie she told herself was that it gave her something to do, but she felt a discernible difference when she put them against her skin. She knew the difference when she did a load of towels, using the soft liquid or the powdered detergent to wash them. She knew the scent and texture of when they had been dried on the Hills hoist and bathed in sunlight. Surely sunlight had a smell. The rays of yellow light hitting the material as it dried in her garden. Pollen and insects and grass clippings of the garden, but surely sunlight did something to the fibres. Sometimes she used Sunlight, a yellow soap, to make them smell nicer, but as her face pressed into the towel, she thought about how the UV rays here imprinted them with a freshness. Oh, what of the luxuries of home. Oh, what of the things that could be controlled. In the world, that was something for her. Just for her, these simple things, like the feel of sunlight-dried towels. She needed to impart this to Resurrection, that the troubles of the world would always intrude, but she could gain a form of control in her home and her attitude to the work.

After drying her face with the towel, the Nivea tin was in front of her like a monument. She realised she wanted her husband gone for good, but she could not say it aloud yet. He had helped with the conception of these two very wanted children but now she realised she did not need him. He would disappear, sometimes for months at a time. Say he was going to Greece, and she wondered what kind of man would leave a mother of two—that did not drive, mind you—for seven months of the year to go and live back in the village. She had got into the habit of drinking two longnecks a day. She would put the kids to bed and then get to work, drinking after all the chores had been done. She drank, sitting at the kitchen table, TV on low, the murmuring filling up space. If she was lucky, there would be a movie to watch. But it was not fun. The drinking just helped her sleep. And she would always sleep on top of the covers and blankets. Once, she had done her nightly ritual and woken up late and the children were not in the house. The beer bottles she had left on the kitchen table were not there. Her daughter's bed was made but her son's was not. Their schoolbags were gone. She opened the fridge, the lunches she had made them had been taken. It seemed the older girl must have got the younger one ready and taken him to school. She never mentioned it to the girl. She just made sure that whenever she had a drink to commemorate her absent husband, she would put an alarm on to wake herself extra early so that she could dispose of the bottles herself. Make sure the children would never see them again. It was a pattern she told herself she would not repeat, but then night would come, and the darkness was a song that lured her.

The day was beginning to feel like a labour and it had not even started. She wanted to clear her head and went to the kitchen to have a cigarette with her Nescafé. She looked at the laminate kitchen table, her eyes taking in the creeping light. It was as clean as she had left it last night, apart from the longnecks. The table shone with its plastic cover and that morning sun, her favourite light, coming through the lace curtains. There were two VB longnecks, both empty, casting a shadow of brown elusive shapes onto the table. After the biscuits, after the cigarette, she would put them away.

She turned on the kettle and stood at the gleaming sink. All the dishes were in the rack. One day she would get a new kitchen. She dreamed about the ways she would improve the place if she had money. First, she would put in a sliding door that would go from the kitchen to the television room, or put an arch right there. She did not know how, but she would make it better, all the Greeks that did well had a lovely arch in their house. She would redesign the kitchen so there would be more space, a long bench so she could do things. It would be easier to make spinach pies, to roll out long handmade dough and use the gargantuan stainless-steel bowl to mix the bought and gleaned greens. Perhaps she could install a countertop that went all the way around the walls, surrounding her with pots, pans, breads, teas, and kettles. The water finished its boil. She exhaled in conjunction with the kettle and poured the water over the granules.

On the sill of her kitchen window were some Holiday Menthols and a crystal ashtray. She got the ashtray down, opened the kitchen door. The cigarette lit, she breathed in the plumes of smoke, it went all the way down into her throat, constricting the muscles, warming her inside, releasing the chemicals, which made her think of all the tasks she needed to do today. Her thoughts went to her mother, those early times in the hut in the mountains, how her mother would wake to a sleeping house, keep the house clean, and spoil her—a victory wife. All those times when she would be the one attached to her mother's brown skirt, her body collapsing when she was not allowed to touch her, so much so that her mother, who would be busy filling the stove with firewood, would have to stop and spoonfeed her some cherry jam and basil. The freshness of the cigarette, the menthol, made her click her mouth together and push up her tongue, reminding her to eat something because the day was going to a big one.

If an ancestor was looking down upon her now, would that father, may God protect and keep him, see her in the kitchen and see her restless soul? It felt like her inner parts would always stir and she wondered what they would say about the betrothed or her offspring. Her eyes went to the side, looked down into the corner. Spirits and our ancestors do not see us that way, she thought. They do not see inside cupboards, our unordered lives. They could not see that she had accidentally put the rice next to the cans of conserved fruits. No, she thought, this is not the way past ones see me. No, the ancestors, floating around—her grandmother whom she had never met, her father who had passed—well, they would not care in the way she would have. They would look at her mind, see the distress, see the way her thoughts wrestled and folded upon each other. What would they say to her? What would they tell her to do to fix it? Be calm. Give yourself some peace. Let go, and understand that so much of it, the conflict, is not within us. Forgive yourself for your transgressions, because we have become something we cannot control, something that is larger than us, the forces, the spirits, the energies we encounter, of which we stand in the way and cannot get out of. She said this prayer as the smoke went in and out of her. She said this prayer to solve and absolve all the things that were wrong with her. She said this prayer, offering grace upon herself and inhaling the last of the menthol cigarette. It went into her breath like it was the spirit of church itself, like she was a part of God Himself and she saw it, the light of the sun, enlivening the vapour, lighting it up in twirls of sunlight and God.

She finished the cigarette and squashed it into the crystal ashtray, she could not get lost in her thoughts anymore. The first thing she needed to do was iron the boy's garb. He would be wearing the traditional soldier's uniform. It was a three-piece outfit she had asked to borrow from the archives of the church. They were lucky to have it. By her watch, the time was getting closer. She knew the skirt would be the hardest of the things to iron, she would have to give individual attention to each pleat. She placed the ashtray back on the sill and next to it the packet of cigarettes.

The ironing board was behind her bedroom door and the iron was in the linen cupboard. She set herself up to work in front of the television. Her son's uniform was hanging in his room and when she went in there to get it, he did not stir. She plucked the uniform off the doorknob.

The blouse that was part of the uniform was puffy, made of a linen cotton material. When worn, it was loose and hung away from the skin so she figured it would not need any work. She picked up the red vest made of velvet and contemplated the dazzling sewn-on embellishments. She did not see any flaws in it and realised it would be better left untouched. She was afraid of ruining this garment that did not belong to her. She turned her attention to the skirt. It would need to be done delicately. It was all white and it needed to be ironed from the inside out. Her iron sputtered and coughed. She did not know why but it was not working properly. Her brow creased, thinking that she might ruin the clothes, but she could not afford another iron. The resentment in her grew. Her husband had gone to Greece for seven months and she could not afford an iron! She burned her way through her thoughts but gently oh so gently ironed each row, each pleat of the skirt. Row by row, iron moving parallel to the lines, the metal glided and steam rose as the iron wheezed. The skirt was taken care of, despite her not having the right equipment.

Just as she was finishing the final pleat of the skirt, the phone rang. She turned the iron off by pulling the plug straight out from the socket. She said it aloud—an incantation that was helpful to remember. A call this early indicated it was going to be the husband.

She shifted her body to the phone bench and sat on the vinyl seat. The phone rang again, she took a breath and picked it up, expecting her husband to yell through the crackling tone of an international call. It was his sister, Prophetess. Her voice had been forgotten and a name was needed to place who she was.

Prophetess was the one she had bought the cow's milk from after finding out that her mother-in-law had been spitting in the goat milk and trying to hex her son. Mostly she remembered the kind gesture of Prophetess giving back all the money she had spent buying the cow's milk. This gesture was the most generous gift that anyone in her husband's family had ever given her. They had initially bonded because they both did not get along with the matriarch of the house. But this gesture, the gift that had been given with foresight, had bound them. It was overwhelming, she held the receiver to her ear and her eyes became watery.

The last time she had seen her, they had been alone and stood facing each other, her fingers on her forearms. Her breath had been shallow, only reaching to the top of her chest, and she had felt her collarbones constricting against her shirt as she looked into Prophetess's unfortunate eyes. She had to look away because she knew the feelings could not hold. And standing there, in Greece, on his side of the island, the land had expanded around them, the soil underneath the soles of their feet connecting the sisters by marriage. And a pact was made.

She was his much older sister and there had been three siblings that had died in between them. What had that done to them? What was it like to know that one was born a girl and then to have three girls die after you in mysterious ways? Such grief and unresolved questions. It was quite possible that no other relationship could have formed after this, the questions leading to a vast unresolved emptiness. Prophetess had taken on the role of mother to Honoured's husband until she stopped being a mother to him when her own daughter was born. Then she did not want anything to do with him. And for some reason, no one could understand why, they stopped talking altogether. Honoured attributed the feud to family character. She tried to fish around, to cast a net to find out why, but both parties obfuscated the answers.

And now to receive a call from her. She sat next to the phone, listening to the unexpected voice from the past. And all the memories rumbled inside her, like little unexpected earthquakes that the white rock island was known for. The voice that said hello crackled and fizzled in the rupture of international lines, the wires and satellites there to keep them together not working. So, she looked outside the window as she talked. There was his garden, with the plants he had illegally brought into Australia from Greece by carrying little seedlings in his shirt pockets through customs.

Honoured said the kids were yet to wake. Her teaching work was going well and she was looking forward to working at the library soon. The phone crinkled in her ear and she found out that the daughter of Prophetess was to become a teacher as well. She listened to updates of her sister-in-law's life, a part of her wondering why she was calling. Had he died over there? Would she have to be a widow and publicly grieve? Would she have to walk around the streets of Belmore wearing all black and let people see her and know that she was without a husband? Sympathy in waves at her feet, sympathy made real in grieving gifts and candles and aromas of aniseed and orange wafting through the house. No, they kept talking pleasantries until she was ready to announce the unwelcome news.

Prophetess spoke to her with care, she hummed the information, and it was delivered with an air of reluctance. I am sorry, you may or may not know, but he has been with the town women. Particularly one widow. This information was not new to her. She had already heard about this from her own sisters, who had been informed by someone in his village. She had even been told that one of the women was an old widow, as if the age of the woman would shame her. She knew and did not care. Let them have him. For what could she do. She would drink again. She knew that. At the end of the day, after the kids had gone to bed, she would pull out a longneck or two. She thanked Prophetess for the information and said it was something she would need to think about.

She stood up and walked around. She was shaken, but the feeling was familiar to her. It was like the house was his scrawled handwriting, a giant cursive gesture. She looked at the walls and there he was, in the way he had painted them. He had done the job himself to save money, but he had not done it well. He was not a professional and like every task he did, he had got bored, rushed to finish it, distracted by other things. There were paint drips on the walls, long eggshell-coloured tears frozen in time. Something unnamed and unrecognisable came from the back of her spine and reached over her. Sometimes, if she let it, everything around her turned into him. The wooden doorframes too. He had sanded them down to make them as smooth as possible and had used a varnish over them of his own making, mixing an inky red in with the clear lacquer, making the wood look like it was tinged with blood. Why was she reminded of blood? There was too much of him here. She went to move away from the room, to see what would happen. The room itself was ready to cry. The room was going to turn into something else, she had to get out of there. She went into the living area where she thought she saw him standing. No person there, just the coffee table, assertive in the middle of the room. The bottom of the coffee table was wrought-iron in a floral pattern. Metal flowers expanded up and around. Florals, usually soft decaying delicacies, forged in the hardest material imagined. Because the glass top had been destroyed, her husband had replaced it with a window from an old train. The edges of the train window still had the rubber encasement and parts of it were chipped. The painted walls, the doorframes rendered in his own colours, felt like they were closing in on her. Her skin felt the presence of his hand on the side of her face, like something hitting the top and bottom of her cheeks at once, and she exited the room.

This exceptional information required another cigarette. Since that morning menthol, another life had unfurled and now she needed to get back into the order of things. Find her patterns and her ways. She needed to rid her mind of the doorframes that ate her up, and that crying wall paint. She had to think about the day, the students standing on stage at the church hall and reciting their badly written speeches about the importance of March 25th. Last year she had to get to the hall early to pull across all the accordion doors and hide the classrooms from the community of parents waiting to see their children perform. How the parents had judged them all that day. Last time, she had been so scared about what the Belmore parish would think about her that she had hidden behind one of those accordion doors and held a remote mic to announce each student.

She found herself in the kitchen again. As the sun fell through the windows, she saw the trees stirring outside, the light cutting into shapes. She stood in front of the kitchen bench with her children's lunchboxes. And she wondered what would happen to the food she would pack for them. They would be out, hungry, and they would ask for something, perhaps they might get excited by seeing an ice cream truck and ask for money to get a cone. Money she did not have. The young one had only recently started to understand that they could not afford things and lucky for her she had not been the one to break it to him.

One day when the three of them had taken the train to Bankstown Square, the boy had whined and stomped his feet, said he wanted a certain toy, his voice becoming ridiculously hard, his voice becoming the kind of whine that she would not hesitate to smack out of his mouth. But as he complained and untethered her, she had been surprised when Resurrection pulled him into line. Her daughter grabbed her brother by the hand and almost pulled his arm out of its socket and said to him, Listen, do you not understand? We cannot afford it. We cannot afford all the things that you want. So you need to stop. Okay? Because we do not have money. And the son did not even look at her, because she was too busy pretending that she had not heard it. It was such a relief that it was her eldest who had broken that news to him. No, it could not be the mother to tell the child that they were poor. Of all things to do, that was not one of them. No good could result in a mother breaking a son, a male spirit, giving them a dose. This boy, her dead brother, and her dead father, may God protect and keep them.

She put her palms on the melamine bench in front of her. The fake wood grain pressed against her fingertips and a cool feeling ran up her arms from the synthetic countertop. She used her neck to turn her head this way and that, shaking her brain to forget about the morning's news. From the basket she got two apples and turned on the faucet, she held their green skins under the running water. Water streamed over the apples, curving around them, and plunged into the sink.

PART 5
2017

CANTERBURY HOSPITAL
HONOURED CITIZEN

Honoured was lying on a stretcher and an orderly was pushing her through the hallway. All she could see was the ceiling of Canterbury Hospital above her, with its grey fibreboard and fluorescent lights of boredom. She was thinking about the bouquet of Australian native flowers she had received, how the strong dome shape of the waratah had added colour and warmth to the hospital room.

The bed she was lying in was steered towards the Acacia ward. She was wheeled past the front station where she looked to see if she recognised any of the nurses. The hospital bed glided on the linoleum floors. The noise of the rolling wheels was a common sound to her. Hospitals were a part of her life. Wheeled beds and wheelchairs were just domestic furniture now. There was no element in these institutions that could shake her into a new series of emotions, but as age encroached, she was starting to think more and more about these moments in them.

At the end of the ward, the orderly turned the gurney in to the room and parked it next to the bed. She spoke in Greek to the young man that pushed her. She had found out that he was ancestrally a mainlander, from the area of Thessaloniki. She assumed that his mother was a fine baker of sweet breads and pastries. Her tours of that northern city were fresh in her mind. It was a communist heartland and had the finest bakeries bequeathed to the city from its once strong Jewish population. She mentioned that her daughter had taken her to Labour and Socialist museums when they were there. But what she really liked was the bakeries. Oh! The senses and flavours came back to her, emerging at the back of her tongue, the warmth of the chocolate on the roof of her mouth, the crunch of nuts on her teeth, the soft yellow bread floating in her mouth as she chewed it—a pleasured prayer remembered, far from here, in a mountain city. The mouth memory was quickly wiped away by an automated spray of antibacterial air freshener that was mounted on the wall next to the bed.

She had asked the young male assistant if he knew her son and he had cocked his head, making her assume that he did, intimately, more than he would have liked to disclose. His tilted head and too-pristine haircut made her think that her son and this man had once had an intimate transgression. In the park, some darkened street, under a bridge. She didn't ask him again, didn't even mention her son, just talked to the orderly about the three days she had spent at the hospital, how the doctors had sent her for scans of her replaced body parts. She only had septicaemia, she told him. A blood infection that had started in her legs. Downplaying it in hindsight, but somewhere inside she realised the risk it had posed to her life, close to death. When she had first got sick, she had spent days facedown in bed, sweaty skin, thinking she was fine while throwing up undigested Sao biscuits. Only a few days ago, she had nearly died and her son had intervened.

She heard a dramatic metal sound; it was the orderly putting down the side rails on the bed. He picked up one of her legs and moved it across, she sat up and pulled herself onto the bed.

Honoured took a breath and leaned back, asked the orderly to pull the curtain around her bed. The sound of the curtain wheels tracking around her was an end to the morning's events. The curved track also provided some mental shelter from the other patients. She was lucky to be on the farthest bed, next to her a wall with a window that looked over a sliver of a court-yard. In the courtyard was a base of pebbles that went through the one-metre-wide space between buildings and in the middle were succulents that rose out of the rocks. They were plants that didn't need any light or water to survive. Those succulents made her long for the familiar. They powered through extreme weather so they could exist in a little place, in the courtyard of that hospital, just so she could look down on them and be reminded of the cactus out the front of her Belmore home. The orderly asked if she needed anything else, she looked over to him and saw the curve of his chin and hook of his nose. He looked familiar too. She asked him a question that came out as an order. Had she taught him in the Greek afternoon school or served him at the library where she worked? His hands found his pockets, said both might have been possible.

She became distracted when she saw that someone had left her another bouquet of flowers. It really was like a florist in there now! The flowers were in a large plastic cup, which had been previously used and washed out, they were all Australian natives, the two wattles had been dyed to bring out their colour and the leaves had sharp spikes on them. She knew they were from her son; he always bought her Australian native flowers because she loved their odd shape.

She cast back to when her son was young and they had been walking to school. He was in year five and too old to be walking with her, but three days before, a stranger had affected him. She remembered his brown eyes looking up at her, pleading, describing a rusted car with scuffed hub caps that had gone too many times around the block. Inside the car was a bald man. Her boy said the bald man had been looking at him, at his short shorts and the cream thighs coming out of them. Each time the man passed the child, he slowed his car down until the son sensed something strange and started running. Her son told her this, and it inflamed a panic in her. She rearranged her work shifts to make sure she was his paladin against these men. The following day she reluctantly held his hand—was he too old for this?—and they walked to school together and he would break his grasp to pay attention to some of the strangest things. She thought he was unlike other boys his age. So easily distracted and sometimes even skipping while looking whimsically into the air or down on the road. Sometimes he would say, Look at this blue plastic in the storm drain! Why is it down there? And she would reach for his wrist, to hurry him on his way. On the way to his school, there was a house with the loveliest garden. Once he had stood on the low fence so that he could lean his torso over and put his nose right in the roses. Ah, his nose! It was the same round shape as hers and she loved it. Her children had her button nose. It meant they were hers. As she watched the young one inhale the scent of the flowers, she complained about how the roses his father grew only blossomed some of the time, that his father was no good at understanding the complexities of the too-humid weather and the random ongoing rains of Sydney. Her husband spent most of his time in the garden and still the trees were pruned too hard and different weeds occupied the soil amongst the food plants. She hurried her son along, castigating him for dawdling. She realised a long time ago that her son, always closing his eyes to dream, to be distracted by colours and scents, was the opposite of his sister—who, only four years older than him, was a proper guardian. Honoured had pulled her son along, her feelings fluctuating between pushing away his differences to accepting his strangeness. She accepted this strangeness because of the precarious life she had herself, and as they walked past a medium strip of bottlebrushes, she patted her palm on the red bristles and stroked them with the back of her finger. Look here now, she said. Look at how well these plants grow on this land! Look at the loveliness! How the leaves of this plant match the colour of the land! And then walking past the house with the barking sausage dog at the end of their street, she looked at the muted yellow of the wattle flower, its branches reaching to different corners, and she said to her son, No matter how many times I see it, these flowers, will always remind me of the new place where I am, that I am somewhere I have never been before, that I am somewhere so far from home, far away beyond the rolling waves, away from Europe in a world of the tropical. It's like those birds over there—she pointed out an ibis to her son, with its elegant beak and dinosaur head—and he said, Do you mean the dumb bin chicken?

The flowers were obviously from her son. The piece of evidence confirming it was that they had been placed in a rescued plastic iced coffee cup. He always had a coffee in his hand! How much did he spend on iced coffee! Every time she saw him, he held an iced coffee like a prop, or there would be a large iced coffee in his proximity, the cubes melting into a leftover liquid, half clear and half black. There had been other times when he had driven her and she had seen discarded plastic cups in his car, watery ice residue, splashing around the bottom of the container as he turned around corners. Now, if she imagined his stocky silhouette, his arm would be held in front of him and in it would be a coffee like a shield. She had come to associate him with these drinks, so much so that she had bought him a reusable cup so he could make coffee at home, save his money and not leave all these those plastic cups lying around. She understood the appeal of being highly caffeinated but also suspected that his addiction obfuscated some underlying issues. When he had moved back to her house after his breakdown, she noted that his addiction issues manifested through smoking and eating. She pleaded him to stop eating McDonald's, even pleaded to his friends that came over to pick him up: Please! Tell him to stop eating McDonald's! He takes his car through the drive-through! Now, every time she saw him hold that iced caffeinated beverage she had a script: don't-waste-your-money. And he would respond with his script: it's-not-a-waste-it's-fun. And she would say: Oh yes! Lots of fun! I can see all the fun from here! That was the fun that had followed her, she thought, it had followed her, her whole life, all the way from the island village of Katouna to the Australian suburb of Belmore.

She lay in the hospital bed and her whole body heaved with a sigh. She could see the morning light from her window, a pleasant flow she associated with the Australian warmth and those paintings of the lost girls in paintings at the art gallery. Oh! How so much of Australian life was made by women lost in the bush, taken in the bush, and loved in the bush. *Farmer Wants a Wife*. That was a show to watch. And what a show! Another one about the sisters who were also daughters, and they were on the farm and had romance. Oh, that romance. To see love on screen between gorgeous people.

About this time in the morning, family would visit her, those who did not require her affected schoolteacher or librarian voice, those she could speak plainly to or yell at in Greek from her hospital bed. Her son must have dropped off the flowers before an early morning shift at his work and he would now be driving through Belmore. She loved living in Belmore. She was jealous of the sights he would see! She had a fondness for its nature strips and the three giant pine trees just near her home. Hands reaching to the sky. It was curious how the patterns of the grass on nature strips had written themselves into her mind. She thought about the church they lived near called All Saints, with its Byzantine dome, and brought her fingers together and crossed herself three times in reverence. But what she really loved about her home suburb was all those places that were part of their lives, the houses of each Greek family she knew. Over there in the double-storey house with the lemon tree out front were the Three Rose family. They might have a gay son too, but they would never speak of it. Over in the single shack with the lavender bushes was the widow Farmer Digger and her two daughters. She passed them in the map of her mind, the roads leading to the primary school where her children went. Along the streets were her places of employment, the library and childcare centre. Her mind settled onto her father's face, his full head of grey hair and hand-rolled cigarette, waking from a midday nap. He was long dead now, but his influence still hung over them, the bull swimming in the Pacific.

She was luckier than the other Greek women around her. Would think herself smarter than the rest of them if her vanity allowed it. She had had wonderful workplaces compared to them.

The local Canterbury Council, who had paid her to work in its childcare centres and libraries. She had worn the blue uniform and would pat the insignia before a shift start or even walking around her neighbourhood. And Belmore's proximity to the public hospital had made their families' working lives so much easier. Visits to the hospital had increased in frequency, especially in her later years. A crumbling body and her son's crumbling mind, and her daughter's three births. All coinciding with her hair greying and retirement. These visits to medical institutions had been milestones in her life, she went there when she needed scans, when she fell over and needed knee replacements. This area was more than a hospital though, the main street of Belmore was ribbon development, the rows of delis, bakeries and nut vendors creating the warmth of light in her. She wondered if the sunlight hitting the courtyard outside her hospital window was pouring its rays onto the Hellenic baker, where she bought the white sourdough loaves she had been buying since the nineteen-eighties. One of the traditions from the island was to have bread with every meal, even when they ate a rice pilaf. Double carbs! her daughter would exclaim. Over the years she would send one of the kids to go to the shops and buy the bread that was mandatory for their dinner table. When her children returned with the white paper bag filled with loaves and rolls, she would put the bread on the white melamine board, slice it back and forth with a long knife, take a gorgeous white piece and put some MeadowLea on it—the oil and fluff providing the perfect accompaniment to a hot cup of black Nescafé.

Just as her memories of bread were feeding her, one of the food servers from the hospital wheeled in a cart, interrupting those carb pillow dreams. She saw the big metal box on wheels, the expectation of lumpy sadness making her reflect on how there could be no nutrition in the pre-packed hospital food. The server placed the tray of food on her side table and swivelled it over her lap. Honoured made sure to look the young woman in the eyes. Under her brown pools were thick black circles. She recognised a new mother, thanked her for the food and did not make any complaints about it. Looking down at the plate she kept what she thought of it to herself, applying the protocols of being a guest in someone's house. She would not break the column of tradition that informed her behaviour. The Greek concept of hospitality, friend of the foreigner, in the architecture of her thinking. Added to this was the respect she had for workers from her Labour politics. She was thankful for the worker's gesture and the unappetising plastic compartments that had been served to her. In the corner of the tray was a slice of brown bread wrapped in plastic that crinkled, on top of it was a pat of margarine wrapped in yellow-branded packaging that would make anyone question if there was any place that was free of advertising. Next to it was some flavoured Greek yoghurt. Although she preferred flavourless Greek yoghurt, this one had strawberry jam strewn through it and it would be her favourite part of the meal.

She was reminded of George Hussein, who she used to have lunch with when she had worked at the library. One time she watched him eat from a large Attiki container of yoghurt and shouted at him: Hey! Silly old man! The clumps mean that it's gone off! He laughed at her and said there was rice in it. She interrogated him further. Rice? Really? In yoghurt? The simplicity of those two staples. Her mind had run an inventory of her fridge and pantry at home, wondering when she could next combine those two things.

This hospital visit she missed rice and yoghurt. That simple dish. And in this post-work life she missed the camaraderie of lunch with the people she worked with. Next to the yoghurt was an embarrassing clump of yellow that attempted to be scrambled eggs. She ignored it and instead unwrapped the bread from its packaging, the crinkling of plastic like tiny explosions. She tore the slice up and peeled back the lid of the yoghurt in a smooth gesture. She quickly dropped torn bits of bread into the yoghurt, still hungry from the big morning of scans. Bringing a spoonful to her mouth, she sensed the dairy goop drop on her chin. She became more deliberate with each tear and dip, shutting her eyelids to sense the food in her mouth. The plain bread and sweet yoghurt, the combination of fluffy and creamy she loved so much. Her hunger wasn't satiated and she thought about escaping the hospital, making a dash to the closest KFC.

Different relatives had come by—sisters, in-laws, first and second cousins—bringing many gifts. Most unthinking guests had brought her Ferrero Rocher or Toblerone. But she loved the assorted boxes of Celebrations that contained all the Mars-branded confectionary treats. The variety was surprising. She could justify to herself that a Cherry Ripe was just as delicious as cherry jam and when she bit down on it, she was a child again, smelling the cherry jam of the island, eating a spoonful with a basil leaf on top. Mini Bounties, with their white and flaky centre, had the meat of a coconut and tasted healthy to her. Family members who knew her likes went all the way to her favourite Lebanese nut roasters on the main strip of Belmore. They brought her bags of salted pistachios, dry-roasted almonds, and cashews. There were mixed roasted nuts hidden away in the drawers next to her bed. Next to the nuts were sultanas clumped in clear plastic bags, so it looked to her that there was brown dirt sitting in the drawers. She loved dried grapes. She bought them in such large quantities that she had started putting them in the cakes and sweet pies that she made. They became so common that her daughter started having an aversion to them. And her husband and son started to look down on the milk pies filled with the dry fruit and groan at the thought of it being fed to them. But she loved that guests to her house knew that she would be serving a tea plate full of sultanas with their whisky and Coke.

She rummaged through the plastic bags and picked out some sultanas. Her mind stepped back in time to a few days ago. She was sitting in the kitchen and their guests had just left. She was watching her husband dispose of the plates of sultanas straight into the bin. He hit the edge of the plate against the plastic edge, and each time the dried fruit would rain in. Each tap against the bin became needlessly hard. He started mumbling. His anger started to grow. At first, she would flinch at the gestures, the speed and sound recognisable to her, she knew it as a harbinger. He was cursing the guests that had just left. It started with some words uttered in a terse tone. Idiots and morons and fuckwits! And as his voice escalated to a crescendo, he threw the whole plate in the bin, looked up to face his wife, pointed at her and yelled.

The guests that had just left were nicknamed Shaken Woman and the Dragon Mumble. Shaken was so beaten and terrified of the man that eventually her voice had disappeared. She would speak in fragments and answer in one or two words. When Honoured thought about her, she thought about the sounds that came from her mouth and the series of shakes that would appear at the slightest hint of confusion or conflict. He was the Dragon Mumble, called this because his big lips would clumsily collapse around his muffled speech. But from the impression of his anxious wife, they knew that Dragon Mumble could breathe fire. She had never seen the dragon—extended mouth, canines out, the flicker of the flames. Dragon Mumble kept to the strict protocols of Greek face: be someone else in public and something else in private. But his opinions were so stupid that they would enrage her husband. And it would bring out the unsettled horned beast in him. Just as they had all sat sipping their Johnnie Reds, Dragon Mumble had gone off on his new favoured rant: Albanians in Greece. Her husband tried to stop him. He had friends that were Albanians. One of his child's friends he called The Kosova. He said to him: Stop! You fool! Don't you remember when we came here? You have amnesia? Have you seen the Albanians speak to their children in Tosk and the children reply in Greek? Now who does that remind you of? Dragon Mumble said something about the Greek news and repeated a parroted line made up from the worst of their people. This had infuriated Honoured's husband so. When her husband looked up from the bin, with its discarded plates of sultanas, he yelled at his wife about how stupid the Dragon Mumble was. She pushed back; you know what he is like, why do you engage him so? It escalated him and he left the kitchen, yelling through the house.

She pulled up one of the hospital bedsheets, kept putting sultanas in her mouth and chewing. Her mouth moved in pattern, her hand rhythmically putting in another, then another. Outside the window the sun still pierced the courtyard, wanting to warm her bones. Warming her bones. A saying. Oh, the way the Greek words sounded in her mind. The Greek word for bones was part of the literature of her nation. The national hymn came to her, Greek people were recognised from bones, exhumed from the earth. Oh, to warm my bones in the hot Australian sun! she thought. These fluorescents won't do it! I cannot warm my bones in this hospital! The aarons of light falling outside would be the same ones hitting Belmore. She thought about the sun shedding his light on the main drag of Burwood Road, the line of light rising until it made its way to Al Rabih Fresh Coffee and Nuts.

The sign on the awning had Arabic letters, but the graphic font on the windows had the Greek and English words for cheese, olives, oil, coffee, nuts, and beans. The shop had been there when she had moved into the suburb, it was still there now. Inside, she took pleasure in the mounds of nuts, legumes, and pulses. She loved excavating the products using the scoops in the plastic tubs. Three bags to last a year. Olive oil in four-litre bottles. There were Turkish coffees she didn't like. Those decadent Ottomans, their too-fancy coffee, too rich in aroma. Once she had even purchased some with cardamom in it and it had to be thrown out so they could go back to their sweet roasted mud. She would speak to the Arab men running the shop, they were compatriots, and their aggressive joviality made her feel welcome: Oh! Here she is again! Our sister! It was this she missed as her mobility had started leaving. When her legs began to make it hard for her to go to the shops by herself, she would make whoever was driving make a quick stop to buy something. Oh! We are just going past! Can't you just stop here for a bit? she would ask. Let me look inside! I need something here. She missed the Arabic men in that shop. Their familiarity with her and their fast-talking mouths, it was a comfort because so many of the men in her life had too much to say but said nothing. All those Mediterranean men that were her friends throughout the years, like George at the library, the nut shop men, and even her husband. All born overseas, always motormouthed, the colour they injected in their lives was permanent.

Her hospital bedsheets were folded over her legs, over her regressions. Around her were the sounds of whirrs, whistles, and beeps of hospital machines. One of the other patients in the room was playing morning television and the voice of the upbeat presenter Samantha Armytage could be heard.

A few days ago, when the blood infection had started in her leg, she thought it was the heaviness. She had felt a slight tingle, but she had difficulty paying attention to it. She had known this heaviness her whole life. When she had worked, she might be standing behind the information desk and feel a pressure coming down onto her head, onto her shoulders, she would feel the bottom of her eyes dragging her face down. Sometimes this heaviness and pressure would be felt the whole day, sometimes it might come on a Sunday morning while she vacuumed the carpet. She took pride in being able to distract herself from it. On workless days she would pull the sun-blocking blinds across the room and lie on top of the doona. Being away from people relieved her affliction of heaviness. This heaviness came and fell on her head, just above her eyebrows, and the feeling would turn into a wave eroding other parts of her away, the parts where she would bake a moist sultana cake or watch her favourite Greek soap opera. Longing for that darkened room, no light, so she could lie there, because the plates inside her would feel the gravity, the plates under her clavicle bones, inside her ribs. And in the daytime darkness, lying on top of the bedspread, the heaviness would release in her eyes, the sides of them moistening, geysers letting out all the pressure of what was in her body. Then she could sleep. Ten minutes or so. And be rested enough to put together some things for dinner. When the children were younger, she had felt lucky at these times. The girl would study, the boy lived in his imagination. Oh, what a relief it was that the youngest had a tub of toys and the daughter was in her books and her husband tinkered. They would be fine without her. She could just shut it, let the heaviness take over.

When there had been a slight tingle in her leg and the heaviness arrived, Honoured thought it would pass with sleep. I just need some sleep and I will be okay, she had said to the darkened room and the emerald pillow covers. She imagined that she would wake up afterwards, open the curtains to let light in and eat a plate of wilted bitter greens with oil and lemon. Some browned toast eaten dry might be nice too, it might offset all that she had been throwing up into the bucket placed next to her bed. And if she was lucky, someone might bring her a wash-cloth to keep her forehead moist. This heaviness in her head was something that needed to be slept away, rested, like it usually did. Two days into the illness, her son had come to put her in the hospital. Only then did she realise that she could have died. He had shown up in his work uniform and her eyes had been two slits, she couldn't even see him. From her bed, she heard him call the hospital. Repeating the story over and over to different people on the phone. Speaking to emergency patient transport. Two uniformed emergency drivers came. They put an IV drip in her arm. She got better and gave them chocolates for their help. They were nice, Australian types, a boy and a girl, although her son had spent too much time looking at the boy. They wheeled her from the house into the back of a van. The van took her to the hospital and a doctor saw her and then another kind of nurse hooked up some other kind of saline into her. As soon as they hooked up her arm the throbbing pain stopped, and her head became cool to touch.

Three days later she was still in the hospital, getting better thanks to sultanas from Al Rabih and saline from Canterbury Hospital. She looked at the flowers that she didn't buy herself, the native ones in the plastic iced coffee container from her son. Despite these gestures of his affections, it was her daughter that she was connected to most. Ever since she had held her as a baby and watched her cry, she saw a determination that was unchanged through the four decades of her life. They shared similar temperaments, both had critical intelligence unlike the men in the family. Both her husband and son were too fanciful, heads in a dream state. Most importantly, her daughter knew what it was to be a woman, one of the worst treated things alive. She wondered when her daughter would come home. She had left Australia for the holidays with her three children and husband and gone to Whistler, Canada, what she had called 'the other Anglo colony'. She thought of the three boys in the snow and ice, exercise turning their cheeks pink, how she loved those boys, for that was what they were—boys that had not become horrible men. Their running speech and babbling mouths still had the endearing curiosity of a child, unlike the charmless dominance of a self-important man.

She asked about them every time she spoke on the phone to her daughter. Resurrection! How are the children? Are the three fighting again? Her daughter was spending most of her time inside the cabin they were renting. She had no interest in slaloming down a mountain. Honoured had to explain the point of skiing to her. Her daughter's in-laws claimed it was part of their Viennese heritage. As natural to them as pumpernickel bread. The Viennese Jews could ski before they could walk. And if anything was so vaguely deemed a cultural tradition, part of a rich practice of heritage, it could no longer be an indulgence like most snow activities were.

Honoured prided herself on the way she was involved in raising those three little boys. It was unheard of in modern Australia. The first one was so ingrained in his grandmother's language that when he had started going to preschool, it was assumed he was deaf and slow based on his inability to speak English. The second one looked so Australian, but he had a filotimo that was uniquely of the culture. Then the third one came, her heart reconstituted when she saw that this one had the darkest features of the three. He had eyes that changed colour like her husband's. It was decided that the third child would be read to in both languages by his grandmother. Number three ended up speaking English with a Greek accent, shortening all the vowels and unable to round his mouth. And these were the jewels she waited for. A Christmas without children. No wonder she got sick, she thought.

She split the shell of a pistachio nut with her sharp thumbnail. The nut exploded out of her grasp and the pieces bounced on her bed then dropped to the floor. The sound they made raining down, one after the other, was the twanging of the bouzouki, each string plucked, shells falling, the strings falling right into her heart. A song of melancholia stirred her. 'When a woman is born, so is her pain,' went the lyrics. Honoured's song rang out, jumping from her birth to the ongoing marriage to her husband. She thought herself burning, each interaction of her life in song was hot oil being poured on the fire.

Pain in her body connected to the pain of her past. After her time in Australia in the seventies, she had decided to move back to Greece. On the island, she had stayed with her younger sister called Light, who at the time was a young communist organiser with the nurses' union. She had lived in the centre of the town of Lefkada, sleeping on her sister's spare bed and taking the bus to see her ageing parents. Bored and unsure of what to do with her life, she wandered. The whole island and the main town had become a place of worship for so many tourists, especially Northerners, who she found cold in attitude and cold in spirit. Many ashen-blond heads came on the summer plane service directly from England. She saw that the British still walked around like they owned the Ionian islands, acting like the place was still under their protectorate, creating their desire to get drunk and messy. She watched the Northern European tourists trawl the main streets, towering over the locals, pale skin and blond hair, in their neutral linens. Watching the Anglos from

Britain, not knowing how to drink alcohol with food, perplexed when they sat down in tavernas, perplexed when they shamed themselves falling in the gutter. Honoured became bored of watching these men and women behave like this. She asked her sister for tasks. Go speak to this contractor about my house. Go to the monastery that we call That Which Is Revealed and pray for what will be revealed to you. So, she did, taking a bus all the way up the peninsula on the island. It was sunny along the road by the beach. Through the window of the bus, she looked out to the sea, into the distance where the blue water bled into the sky. There were clouds far away, and over the rocky sea she saw a waterspout, a sea tornado, winding, connecting sea and sky, spinning to the heavens. She got off the bus and walked all the way to the monastery called That Which Is Revealed. The entrance had a limestone gate, wrought-iron doors and above it was a Byzantine picture of Mother Mary with the child Christ. Mother Mary wore a blue covering and had her arms out, welcoming Honoured. The door squeaked as she entered. She wandered through the building. It had a courtyard full of food plants, she recognised the lemon and olive trees, the scent of mint and basil. The walls had a white render upon them, they were effortlessly clean and framed by railings and columns made of varnished timber. She walked through the courtyard and found the narthex. The concrete walls were painted light blue. There was wooden furniture carved with leaves and aprons on edges and knuckled arms that had been painted over with gold. There were icons as old as Christianity itself hanging on the walls. In the divine room she stood and took an inhale of her life. She picked up two candles and lit them. One for herself and another for the sufferings of her own mother. She asked for Mother Mary to intercede and reveal. She remembered looking into the flame of the candle that she had lit for herself as it burned. She remembered how it had held its outline, but there was a halo of distortion around it where the fire met the air, and in this burning was where she lost her language and the words fell out of her in reverence.

Back then, Honoured realised people saw her as restless. But she wasn't restless, she just wanted to make something for herself. She had started a degree in Athens but hadn't finished it. Went broken-hearted to Australia, thinking there would be a life of her own there, a full realised life with a husband and a family. Instead, she had found herself living parallel to both her older sisters' lives. When she wasn't working in factories, she was taking care of her nieces. She looked after them all. A spinster aunt and cheap babysitter. It was a watercolour copy of a life she had wanted for herself. She knew how to be around the baby nieces, pushing them in toy cars, reading them books, it was a joy. She knew that if she stayed in Australia, there would be more job opportunities, there would be employment, but she would always be an appendage to her older sisters' lives. She would fall into the trap of mistaking both their lives for hers and never be fully realised.

One day, while she was sleeping on her sister's sofa in Lefkada, she had been tasked with depositing money in the bank for a cousin who was doing their mandatory military service. She decided it would be nice to go for a wander. She went down to the main street of the town on the island and slipped into the bank—it was then That Which Is Revealed showed her the living image of an icon. Inside the bank, she had stood in line and in front of her was a man, he wore a navy wool gabardine jacket which hung off his shoulders and tapered into his waist. He looked to the side and she saw his face in profile, it was his nose that stung and fired her up. It was too big for his face, the ridge of it was broken and its tip went down, a hook with sharp angles. His skin was tanned, brown with tinges of gold like the figures of the Byzantium icons. And the wave of hair, black and slick, could have been rendered by the paintbrush of a monk. After her mind floated to the images of the icons, she accepted that it had finally, indeed, been revealed.

His skin was dark, oily, and smooth. Much darker than her family, who all had the pale colouring of the mountain Vlachs. She reasoned he had a mix in him, maybe Cypriot, or maybe from Asia Minor as he had the colouring of Midwife Friday in the village. His skin shone in the light, and it was obvious he had a masterful shave, his sideburns were angled on a perfect diagonal. Underneath his navy jacket, a white shirt seemed to pop out in contrast to his brown leathery skin. His choice of colours was a deliberate effect, to make his own features more noticeable. She wanted to say something to him, to begin a conversation. And just as she reached out with an index to tap his shoulder, his name was called by the teller. The reveal was that his name was Honoured too. It was her name but in the masculine form. He took a few steps forward. She watched him talk to the teller and a greased strand of hair fell onto his forehead. He tried flicking it back up, but it wouldn't stay, he put it back in place with a finger and she noticed his hands. They were broad and flat, clean with calluses on the fingers. He turned to see her watching him. He winked at her. When he turned back to the teller, he lifted the sack he was carrying and pulled out a stack of drachmas and counted it all out for the teller, slowly and deliberately. He had slow and confident gestures. The way he lined up each note next to each other indicated that he had a fastidious attention to detail and there was lots of money. He was rich. The teller counted the money again and gave him a receipt. He took his receipt and placed it in a leather billfold that had stitching all around it. He turned one more time to look at her and walked off. Her name was called by the teller, but she just stood in the spot where he had been. She smelled his fragrance of basil and spice, aromatic yet woody, there was a slight musk and it drifted to the top of her nose. She told the teller she would be back and chased the man outside. She saw his outline in a shop window and called his name. He turned around, tilted his head and walked towards her. I just wanted to say that we have the same name, Honoured said. Oh, he said. Well, I admire that, but we have very different noses. And it was true. She was pale skinned and had a bulbous nose. His nose was ancient and Semitic, it was a temple on his face. He scratched his nose with his pinky finger. On it was a silver ring with a black opal inside. She said to him, in a curious tone: You have been to Australia, too?

Opals. The Australian stone. From the confines of her hospital bed, Honoured thought about how everyone in Australia had these stones. Back then, she had seen them on a man's finger and linked the pretty glitter to the sparkling Sydney Harbour. Now, when she thought about that galaxy-looking rock, she lamented the limestone mountains of her homeland, the dull rock that occasionally glittered. She hadn't seen anyone wearing opal in the longest time. They had lost their lustre when they became associated with the tourists. If only she hadn't been enamoured by the black rock on his pinky, if only she had realised she was being distracted by something shiny. How standing there on Old Road, after chasing him down outside of the Hellenic Bank, her line of sight moving from his nose to the opal ring on his pinky, she should have tried to look more clearly and not fit those things as a gospel sign from That Which Is Revealed. But it was those eyes too, going from grey to blue to green, which were so complex and unnerving next to his skin that they had created a stab of laughter in her. Because no one in her family had those. They were a tribe of black-eyed women, and his changing eyes were like the blue walls of the narthex of the monastery, the grey of the sea tornado emptying up into the clouds, the ash green of the scrub of basil.

She remembered her self-conscious laugh. All of it wrong. One large regret. He was the wrong choice for her. He was the worst. And his eyes had come back to haunt her via the third grandchild, those same 'stop me on the Old Road' eyes that had turned a stab into a laugh. And that was the mess that God had given her? Really? That was the intercession she had prayed for all those years ago at the monastery? To be reminded of this was a hell. Nevertheless, she would love that boy. As she would all those boys, until they started shaving. And now lying there in that hospital and wondering where those three grandchildren were. Across the world in unfamiliar mountains that were different from her own. How cold that air was there! How cold it was here! In this hospital!

She pressed the buzzer for one of the nurses to come help her. While she waited, she turned on the television. Her family kept putting TV credits into the machine so she had ample time accrued. She liked having morning television on in the background. They were discussing the Aboriginals and how they might need to take them away again and put their children into other families. She changed the channel to SBS to see if the Greek news was on. She had a vague recollection of it being on in the mornings, but this was before she had got Greek TV straight into her house.

Before the MySat beamed the dancing weather women of Greek TV to lighten her mornings, she had made a pact to herself that she would never become one of those Australian Greeks who only watched Greek TV straight from the mother-land and had no idea of what was going on in Australia. But the Antenna Pacific channel seemed to be made for her. She watched a soap opera called *Battered Wings of a Butterfly* and when the melodrama of soap wasn't lathering enough excitement, she tuned in to the news and watched the precarious democracy of Greece sway amongst the red flags of the communists and the black shirts of the Neo-Nazis.

The hospital TV settled on SBS, where elegant sounds of Mandarin came out of a Chinese news reporter's mouth. The sounds sharpened the air around her, reminding her she was in a hospital, the recycled air feeling stale to her, like it was not working anymore. She needed the swell of an ocean or the crisp breeze that ran through the Aleppo pines of the home-land. Just as her breath started to sharpen and shorten like the scissor sounds of the Mandarin, a nurse came. Mrs Citizen, how can I help you? said the nurse. Honoured looked up from her hands. Hello there, she said. I'm so sorry to do this to you but can you pass me more of those sheets, I would like to warm up my bones. The nurse went to pass some sheets to her but not before Honoured said, You must be Samoan, eh? And the woman said, No, I am Tongan. And Honoured looked at the woman with Byzantine-shaped eyes, a side part in her hair and a bun tied at the back. Honoured said, Don't worry about it, everyone used to think I was from India when I first came here. I don't know why, I think it was my hair, all black, it went all the way down my back and the people used to stare at how shiny and thick it was and think, oh no, something that thick and black could not come from Europe. It might have been my eyes also. They were black too. With my black eyes and black hair, they thought I was Indian. Which is very far from Greece.

Tonga is closer to Samoa than India is to Greece though. The young assistant passed her the sheets and looked over the chart in front of her. She smiled, cutting her face in half. Honoured was left with her memories of Fina.

Her name was Fina, said Honoured, aloud to no one, revealing a memory she thought lost. The stale air around her was making it harder for the cloud of water to cover her eyes. She could feel the emotions reaching. When she had worked at the library and her two children had both left school, she had found a new moment of joy because there seemed to be so many people who she could become friends with. New opportunities for a deeper inner life opened. She had met Fina, who was the same age as her daughter. As an older woman, Honoured was always excited to have much younger friends than allowed. Young women were drawn to her. She knew it wasn't her wisdom, she would never play the sage, rather she indulged their passions of love and desire, she listened to them when they told her about men and sex. She understood their senses and desires and she lapped up their lives, their unfurling futures, a potential to correct her own mistakes. Being the middle child of five girls meant she could adjust to many different personality types. She liked older women, she nodded at them as she listened and watched them put their hair in grey buns. But the younger ones, she could speak to them and their long curls. And they enlivened her. As did Fina. When they had worked together, they went for lunches and coffees together. Her memories of Fina would always be tied to eating as much as the library. The coldest part of the library was the staffroom. No fresh air or light. A grim eating experience had by all between grey walls on pink vinyl chairs. How come all those big places had the same cold stale air? Honoured's breath became short thinking about it. She remembered standing in front of the staff fridge, ready to microwave a leftover spinach pie, when Fina had walked in for her break. She quickly dumped the pie in the bin. It made a rustle against the plastic liner and a thud when it landed. She held Fina's forearm and demanded that she go with her to the RSL across the park. She didn't even wait for the girl to get her handbag, just dragged her along, pulling her out the door and through the foyer. She was still holding her arm as the auto doors swung open, as they walked across the road and through Anzac Park. They went past the rotunda and all the way to the RSL, where they headed straight to the dining room. They passed the Koreans and Chinese slapping the buttons and playing synthetic roulette. They each ordered a schnitzel, gravy and chips, and sat down at the table.

While they waited for the buzzer to go off, Honoured asked her about boys, even though she knew Fina wouldn't answer. Oh, those island ladies! Oh, they are warm! The younger ones had been taught to respect anyone older than them and she knew it would be hard to break through this, even though Honoured liked this value. Honoured also liked the island ladies because, like her, they said horrible things in the sweetest voice. So many people didn't notice. Honoured remembered the taste of a lemon, lime and bitters as she sat across from Fina at the RSL. To bond with her, Honoured told a story about her daughter who had started dating a Greek boy. She likened him to hollow wood who would never have the oomph required to satisfy her daughter. She remembered Fina peeking over the rim of her Coke, listening to her with glee, wanting more information. So, she told her about her daughter coming into the house one night after a date, wearing her shirt inside out. When she disclosed this to Fina, the trust between them cemented. Fina told her about the Italian boy she was seeing. Her parents said that he was of her world. His parents said that such a Black girl would not do. Honoured lived for the romance, the glint and frisson in the young woman's eye as she spoke about the man she wanted. Fina confessed to the random hook-ups in the back seat of her parents' Tarago and in his small Corolla, their decision to pursue each other in secret. How romantic and enlivened Honoured had felt. Proud that a young girl would disclose this and proud that their unlikely friendship had grown. An older hunched Greek lady and the young Samoan girl. Honoured told Fina to watch out for the Italians, their religion, and their curses.

Honoured held young women dear. And lying there in the hospital, the image of Fina became clearer, it had been a steamy summer and her face had been surrounded by flowering hibiscuses, entombed in a red wooden coffin, surrounded by the wailing parishioners.

As her eyes flickered, Honoured remembered that the mention of Italian curses would summon one from the depths of the Roman catacombs and it made her fall into tears thinking about Fina. Through the blurriness and stale air, there she was in a church where everyone wore black. She heard the call and response of songs, where men sung the low parts and the women sung the high parts, voices mixing like a choreography. She remembered the elderly woman resting at the head of the coffin, how she had wailed to Fina, who had lain so perfectly, so calm, waiting for her Italian boy to attend.

Honoured remembered the young woman she had dragged out of the staffroom. She wept for Fina, the tears going down her cheeks, she wept for herself. She wiped the drops when they reached her jawbone, grateful that the curtain was closed, so that the other women in the room wouldn't see her, would only hear a sigh come out of her mouth and mistake it for the tired breath of an ailing woman.

She liked that hospitals were run by women and full of them. If female staff saw her crying, they would leave her alone. Men acted differently. They would go up to her, fearful and concerned, reach for her shoulder and say, Oh! Honey! What is wrong? or walk away in discomfort. Some men had the energy of her husband but hid it. She remembered crying, his pointed finger, the thunder in his voice, scolding her that there was no need to cry, because those water drops were useless.

This hospital was a place where she could cry. So many female nurses during her stay, from so many worlds. At the front entrance, she remembered that there had been women raising money. They reminded her of all the women in her life, they were confident of themselves and focused on their task. Women in her life were misfits and miscreants she had gathered.

Many of them dating outside their own race and getting married to men who their family didn't approve of. A Greek woman with blonde hair who had married another Greek man—this pairing had been controversial because the woman's sister was married to the man's brother. For some reason, despite there being no blood relation, this was frowned upon traditionally, thus her exile, thus her friendship with Honoured. There were women in their fifties, from different cultures and races, all unmarried. She collected these women, who were bored by the conventions of family, or for some reason had fallen through the cracks. Thank God for Jennifer! She thought of her friend, a Chinese Fijian woman. She was always around; they sometimes went shopping together and sometimes watched TV together. They both understood that men seemed to be obstacles and Jennifer would never ask why her husband spoke in that thunder tone. Or why he would yell at her in front of others. It was an easy life with women. These women who were seen as offcuts.

She was lucky when it came to staying in the hospital. She was grateful to whichever prime minister had brought in Medicare and fought the smug doctors who didn't want it. Something to do with Gough Whitlam, the one who had made Australia multi culture. Ahh! Mr Whitlam, Friend of the Greeks. He was the kind of man who came to their Greek festivals and commemorative days. She had been in Australia when he was in power and had met him twice personally. Apparently, he had made the universities free for citizens, but he also allowed the wogs to be themselves in a way that hadn't been allowed before. He said multi culture! It was okay for them to speak their own language in the street. They wouldn't be yelled at. Told to shut up!

The thing that happened in parliament meant that it was rude for that child—that little one, over there—to walk past the delicatessen on Marrickville Road and hold his nose because he thought the smell was off-putting. That child couldn't smell the freshly delivered bread, the saltiness of the cured meats, the salamis hanging off the counter, he couldn't smell the brine of the feta, he couldn't smell the sweetness of the olive oil or the bitter paprika or the punch of the mountain oregano—the eye of God. Where they got such oregano in Australia, she would never know, it was like it had been plucked from the slopes of Arcadia. So perfect. Remembering it from her hospital bed— the little dry leaves smelling of the valleys—and she was near the pines again, dreaming of homeland, of the motherland, its produce that agreed with her body. She would have been happy eating the ripened figs and bitter olives and fried breads of the home island. But the cracks and sores of that land had made her feel like such a fool. Go away! To the land where the money waits! This command had been to exit the place where they ate the sweet oil semolina pies that made heavy bodies. This command had been to exit the place where bus drivers could stop at the corner shops while on their routes, to pick up milk and fish, because that was their community and the passengers would just wait. Back there, oh how the people there were happy because of the azure, lapis, blue skies, and seas, but it was a trick, because their food had been subsidised with things that they had never understood—the absence of a stable structure of functioning jobs and hospitals. That place wasn't a place for wages or healthcare.

When she had married the man who had the masculine form of her name, Honoured decided that she would work hard towards a good future. She relished the photos that had been taken of them in the photography studios in Marrickville, the area where the Greek community congregated. She missed that rented wedding dress that she didn't keep, her practicality winning over the need to hang a white synthetic dress in her closet that she would never wear again. Like all the diaspora, they didn't know if they were going to settle in Australia or Greece. Or even which part of each country. Down in Tasmania, pregnant with number one, her husband had taken her to the top of Mount Wellington to see if she could drive the Kingswood all the way down, in neutral, engine off. She did it, got her licence and then never drove again. While stuck on that island, she gave birth to her first daughter, who they named Resurrection after his mother. She was happy with the familiarity of her gender. And she demanded that they leave for Sydney to go be with her sisters. In Sydney they lived and ran a corner shop at a beachside suburb called Brighton-Le-Sands. They became friends with everyone. There was an Irish doctor, a woman that lived up the road from them. They became friends with her and had dinner at her messy house, which they allowed because she was a doctor.

Honoured sat upright in the bed, she pressed out her elbows and pushed with her forearms, so she could prepare herself for the next doctor. Getting ready to see what she expected would be a man. Hospitals held memories for her. Boy and girl memories. Two childbirths. Being a child and being taken care of by other women. In these feminine spaces she waited, usually for a male doctor, while the nurses, who knew more about the child that she had birthed or the way her leg was healing, looked on at the side. She always paid more attention to the nurses, especially when the doctor was speaking, their glances revealing more than what a man was reading off a chart. The men who waited to be listened to, each time they spoke, she understood the things they weren't saying. She heard the men who liked the romance of their own voice. Any inkling of that and she would be turned off. A pointless vanity. Not needed anywhere in life. Too much of her husband in that voice. Too much of her son's dawdling. One of the doctors that had visited her was a young man. He must have come straight out of school because he had that plump water skin, morning dew just wiped off. It was the kind of skin you could only have from being too young and too indoors. She thought him polite, the way he caught himself bowing to her. It was a forward tilt from his hip, an angled torso down and his hand reaching to his chest, until he became aware of his bowing. She thought him sweet, endearing, respectful of a grey-haired woman like her who spoke all the English words with an inflection and sometimes in their wrong tense. He had stood at the foot of the bed, his pale blue shirt complementing his skin, and he had held the clipboard with both hands, his fingers placed under it, his elbows flaring out and his neck letting his head sink down. His head seemed to be going into his chest. He squinted his eyes and when he looked up again, he noticed the nurses standing around him, there was one he seemed keen on. The Tongan one. No longer hunched over. His neck erected his head up. He looked her up and down. Honoured's smile went across her face. The Tongan nurse was twice as thick as this skinny boy. But she knew exactly what he wanted. And as he spoke, Honoured started to hate the way he talked. He announced everything. His lips moved around his mouth and the noise came from deep within a part of his chest. But then his hands fell, the clipboard went behind his back. He told Honoured that she had septicaemia. She already knew that, but there was an audience for him now. And he started to fall in love with his own voice. He thought that to impress this Tongan girl, he needed to speak loudly and forcefully, that he needed to point his finger, like it was something that would help him speak well, that it would endear himself to other people. What the nurse would figure out was that he was a man. That he was the kind of person who loved the way he talked. That he loved listening to his voice. The nurse would understand what this quality in a man meant. It was a quality Honoured saw in her husband when he talked at her. He loved to communicate with the sound of his own voice, he stood tall, his hand playing the orchestra. Ra ta ta ta da ta. Singsong, machine gun. She was reluctant to admit that he had a nice voice. That he was someone who could sing pretty and talk pretty. He was a cantor in a previous world, and he loved all things to do with the voice.

And his whistles were sweet too. Some of the sweetest birdsongs any human could make. Though she would not admit it, would never tell him, because he sung for his own pleasure, so he could hear the wails and notes. Her husband spoke to appease the young man, the child inside him that could never be filled. The boy that wanted to be a man. Who thought that being a real man was talking proudly and not listening. This was the male vanity that she despised, that she saw in her husband and now in this doctor standing in front of her.

There were two worlds for her, Honoured thought. One of those worlds was of men who liked their own voices. She had not grown up in it. She had been surrounded by girls, in a woman's world, and had always carried ongoing friendships with them. During her childhood in the village, her mother had quite a reputation for being a bitter and cutting woman. And Honoured was the one that had been closest to her. Upon walking to the markets and meeting a new family, someone would ask her mother how many children she had. Her mother would reply that she didn't have any children, only five girls. This quick response was seen as funny by the person who asked it. They did their uncomfortable laugh. But a pause in thought made them realise that there was something underlyingly bitter, a cruelty to her words. This cruelty, coming out of a woman dressed only in black, who had worn only black for decades after the death of her only son, made her a dark figure. At first Honoured and the rest of the daughters saw this as a slight against their gender, against who they were and what they had been born as. But as time went on, and they discussed things and learned about the quality of men, Honoured thought about it in a different way. 'I don't have any children, only five girls.' Honoured looked up from her bed at the doctor and thought about this statement. What her mother had said had been right. Maybe when she said she had never had children, it was meant as a slight against men. That those men were boys, that they would always be children. Daughters would never be children, they were too mature, too smart, and too wise. Forced to develop in a man's world. Women didn't love the sound of their own voices, in the way that was the vanity of men. She waited for the man to pass, for this peacocking doctor to close his tail and leave the place. To pull that screen back around her, in the room of her mind, framed by these curtains on tracks.

And then she was left alone again, just her and her breath. The nurses had scattered, no longer gathered around her bed. Sounds of a room emptying and the settling of the air around her, that recycled breath of the machines she could hear coming out of the vents. No new air, and she couldn't Domestos or Gumption the place clean. She couldn't put it through the needles of a pine tree to freshen it up. So, she had to imagine herself, sitting under one of those Aleppo pines in the village, leaning onto the bark, feeling its rough texture on her back—hopefully no ants to crawl up the nape of her neck!—and she was up there again. Up in that mountain village. It was setting sun, but it didn't matter because it couldn't cut through the clouds anyway. The winds ran over cliffs through the forests and pushed that fragrant air, scented of greens and dirt and forest fruits. There was a rain falling over the mountain. The pin drops, so fine and light that they couldn't even penetrate the canopy, merely helped the leaves release their freshness.

Christmas time here was one of her favourite times, because of the air. Their single-brick, fibro-walled house was at mercy and—oh wow—the heat washed it in this period. A closed window in summer and that moist heat of Christmas would make the interior of the house indistinguishable from the exterior. Oh, how the eggshell walls would sweat, what glory the visible warmth, to feel the heat warm up her bones. Her mother could never appreciate a hot Christmas. Not their matriarch. All she had known were cold and rainy mountain Christmases. One time in the eighties, the three sisters had flown their mother over to see them in the new land. They had eaten soup together and it had dribbled down their chests. Generations of dribblers all together in the same kitchen. Honoured had seen in her mother a care for winters and the interior of her village life. That she wanted to be up, up there, on the other side of the world, where the land was their bodies, and she could fuss and fiddle over the hand-loomed tablecloths and rugs she had made. Her mother lived by a model of perfection in village life—perfect cook, perfect cleaner—and never let out a scream. The wet and soft and cold things of a life in a village hut. Wrapped up in the material of her clothes, enveloped, layers curling with tiny openings for access points. She knew how her mother gave herself over to all that which was wet, cold, soft, and dark. Five girls, what did you expect from a woman surrounded by the feminine?

As visiting hours approached, she knew that the room would be filling up with too-loud guests and too-loud children (that weren't her grandchildren!). For some reason, the operating manager of the Acacia ward had started putting all the old immigrant ladies into the same room. Of the six beds in the room, three of them were old wogs like herself. The one that had been there a week and had a leg injury like her was a Lebanese Muslim woman. When Honoured first saw her, she had recognised the dark head wrapping as something old-fashioned that female elders in her village used to wear. She called the woman in her ward the same name she would have called them if she had seen them outside in the street, or if it had been fifty or sixty years ago back in the village: Mantillas. It was a reference to the scarf that covered their heads. Whether it was the traditional brown garb of the married Lefkadian woman, the blue of marriage ceremony, or the leopard-print head covering worn by a young Muslim girl—they were all Mantilla. This Mantilla was younger than Honoured, and her family streamed in to visit her from all parts of Sydney. More visitors than what Honoured had. When the curtains were open and all the women could see each other in the ward, they introduced their sons, their in-laws, their grandchildren, their co-business owners, their family friends. Mantilla's name was Fatima. And Fatima, despite her cholesterol, had been given the thick and syrupy baklava from SeaSweet. Pieces of filo pastry with pistachio, covered in syrup and nuts, and in more adventurous moments, stripes of white chocolate, milk chocolate, that would inflame both Mantilla's cholesterol and Honoured's diabetes until they were scolded by the nurses. The nurses told them the sugar syrup was no elixir for women their age and they responded with grand existential statements and declarations: One must die sometime! We all go at one time or another! The sweets were then distributed amongst the women of the ward. And Honoured knew that the newer the arrival, the more the relations, which meant more offerings would be given and distributed. But oh, what happened when Honoured bit into the Arabic baklava. When the gritty nuts held together by syrup cement got caught in between her teeth. When the paper-thin pastry crunched and its crumbs fell on top of her chest. It reminded her of times working in the sugar patisserie. Was that it? Sweets took her back to a time when she had been a girl in Athens. Had her fondness for custard-filled yoyos and soaked rum babas started in an Athenian cake shop? One of the few dishes that she had mastered, which all the family agreed on, was the custard semolina slice. The Greek syllables enunciated in her mind and she mouthed it like a noiseless prayer. Ga-la-to-bou-ri-koh. Secretly adding drops of the orange water that she got from Al Rabih Nuts to make it sing and make it her own. Sprinkling the fragrant Arabic water, bringing out a surprising tang to the dairy, enough to sharpen the flavour and have her sisters eye her suspiciously and say, Well, it's good, but you were always the one that loved sweets! The biggest in the family amongst us all! All that would do was send her in for another spoonful. Was this desire for sweetness really about the sugar patisserie she had worked at? Did each bite make her feel courted again by men? Was each swallow a remembrance of her potential? Masked by the sweetness in her mouth, that pain would disappear.

She looked over to the flowers from that gay son of hers. Crumbs from the filo pie that her sister had made floated in the container holding the bouquet. Three crumbs of deliciousness hovering amongst the stems. As the air conditioning hummed over the flowers, there was a sense of gratefulness that came over her.

Belmore. Sydney. Australia. This was the place she would be buried in. Her bones would meld with this ground. She loved it just enough for this moment.

In this place she could eat the most ornate baklavas and drink gifted ginseng tea from Korean neighbours because she had a curiosity for geography. Access to other cultures began with her tastebuds. When she had first met the Mantilla, she had a curiosity about her wardmate. The most boring questions first. Married? Children? Grandchildren? And then Honoured spoke about her favourite things. How she had worked at the library. She told the Mantilla how much she loved a schnitzel at the RSL. They spoke about bigger events, the wars they knew and the wars they had come from. They confessed the borders they had crossed and the men they had married. In secret they both told each other they loved flowers but would never buy them themselves.

Throughout their days there, the Mantilla had paraded her relatives and grandchildren. Once Honoured had looked up and seen so many children, all alongside the Mantilla's bed, there might have been six or so. Honoured's glee at seeing the children was also confused with pangs of envy that she couldn't show off her daughter and those three grandchildren of hers, which, she surmised, were much better looking than the ones of the Mantilla.

PART 6

2020

BELMORE
RESURRECTION CITIZEN

Resurrection backed out of her driveway and scarecrow was the word of the day. Her mother, Honoured, sat next to her, caressing a grey strand of hair, failing to put it behind her ear. Just as she pulled out of the carport, the caterer's van pulled in. She turned onto the street, leaving a semi-full house, one where the bar mitzvah party was winding down. It was a convenient time to drive her mother home, the caterers needed access to the driveway and her Mum Van was blocking them from getting the empty trays and bain-maries. It was Resurrection's second child's bar mitzvah. Most of the family thought that God was pretentious, a frivolous pursuit, but both boys had wanted to honour their grandmother and their ancestors who had escaped the troubles of Vienna in the forties. Resurrection, who described herself as culturally Greek Orthodox (no time for God!), had organised all the events and food for the families that had come together. That day, she had watched her husband at the party. He drank beers and socialised, he rotated from work group to family groups, from the old Greek-in-laws to the progressive Jews, and to the old gays in the family. He was social, she was practical, and neither of them had found time to eat. When the party had started winding down and her mother rubbed her eyes, Resurrection found the perfect time to drive her mother home and process what was going on.

As they drove, her mother looked past one of the cafes that had sprung up and commented on how busy it was. Why wouldn't it be busy? Resurrection wanted to know. Honoured never expected a business like that to work in Belmore. Not only one cafe but three, she said to her daughter. And restaurants for eating too! This generation! No one eats at home anymore! They drove down the main road, past the old Greek sweet shop. Look at what they've done to it too! Coffees as well! All Holy says they make the best spanakopita that anyone can buy. Resurrection had watched the old zaharoplastio change over the course of living there. When it had first started, it had been an efficient place—come in, buy the cakes you need and wait on linoleum floors while an older woman puts your filled no-frills paper box on an uncharismatic industrial counter! Now there was a display area and a service area. The staff had embroidered aprons as uniforms. Inside, the place was done up with white stone floors and black stools and the outside tables were occupied by old men who loved flipping their worry beads and young men who seemed a race riot away from supporting Golden Dawn. Resurrection was at odds with the gentrification here. It had almost worked, attracting a new and more complex demographic. They wore Gymshark. Their cars were flashier. It remained Greek. But shinier. This cake shop was part of the newly aggressive character to the area. Brought in by the aspirational wogs decked out in activewear who were buying the old homes and turning them into duplexes. It really wasn't gentrification, she thought. It was more Duplexification.

Resurrection was silent in the car. Earlier at the temple, everyone had commented on how much weight she had lost. She didn't care. She intentionally did it so she wouldn't have the same fate as her mother—a double knee and hip replacement. But then her mother had scanned her up and down and told her that she had lost too much weight, that her face bones jutted out. That she looked like a scarecrow. And although she had dismissed it with a shrug, a slight eye roll, the word kept on appearing throughout the day. When she had stood on the chair to make a speech, she had raised a hand. A slight breeze and a crow perched on the fence. That word. She noticed how the breeze ruffled her shirtsleeve, now that it was a size too big. Scarecrow. At lunch she had seen a bain-marie of charred corn and pursed her lips. Scarecrow. Her mother said things that affected her. They always hung around her. Just after the speeches, her mother had summoned her over and Honoured had pointed to her son-in-law. Resurrection looked over to see her husband chugging a Corona. He was amongst a group of men who were chugging Coronas. Her mother said to her: Hey listen, your husband is drinking too much, and people are noticing—with an accusatory finger. Resurrection said it was none of her business. That in fact, she should focus on her own marriage. And her mother said she was just making conversation, that she should be able to say something, to speak, to have a voice. One of her mother's scripts was telling someone that they needed to talk to someone. She instructed others to instruct others.

The bar mitzvah had been at one of the more progressive temples in the city. In the morning she had to calm the second child from his nerves to get ready. She recognised his difficulty as one of her own. After she had wrangled the three boys and her husband into the car, they drove past her mother's house in Belmore, where the boys rearranged their seating so that their grandmother and her walking stick could slide in next to them. Getting her mother into the car had become harder since her two knees and one hip got replaced. Amongst the dog-chewed toys and sports equipment, the six of them travelled to the temple, making their way from the once working-class neighbourhood of Belmore all the way to posh East Sydney. They sped along the highway through the zones of houses and suburbs that had increased in property prices, to the place where hedges became a replacement for fences, and even the apartments had minimal water damage. As they drove, she listened to her mother trying to engage with her grandchildren, but her discomfort and sighs fissured their trip. It was a reminder to Resurrection that maintenance was important, lest the same thing happen to her.

Belmore was slowly passing on either side of them, and her mother picked at her daughter again. She pointed out that she hadn't seemed herself that day. During the bar mitzvah ceremony, members of the immediate family had been called up and asked to say different prayers. When it had been her turn, she got to the podium, looked up and indicated with a slight inflection (detectable only to anyone that knew her) that she had been asked to do the prayer to Israel. After, she went and stood next to her husband. The whole family stood there—three sons, two parents, a grandmother and in-laws—and it was the tiniest of gestures, missed by the whole congregation but visible to those watching closely. Her husband had been standing next to her and reached around to grab her by the waist, and just as he did this gesture of pride and intimacy, she stepped aside, away, intuitively, without even thinking about it.

Later, when the ceremony had ended, she had asked her brother All Holy to come to the Mum Van and help her get some gifts to distribute to the rabbi and divinity teacher. They walked through the foyer next to the synagogue, past the flyers that supported Israel and the rainbow-coloured flyers that supported the gays. She nudged past family members who were mixing with work colleagues. Some of the old neighbours from the temple area weren't going back to southwest Sydney, so impromptu sandwiches and tea had been served post-ceremony. Resurrection and her brother walked out of the temple and through the leafy part of East Sydney. The trees hung over them and the bright autumn day was perfect for her bubble dress. He complimented her on the bright lipstick, and she twirled the bottom of her bubble skirt and said that she had got her dress online and it had pockets! They got to the van, it was parked in between a beaten-down Land Rover and a slick black Audi with a rainbow tassel hanging off the rear-view mirror. The back hatch went up as soon as she pressed the button and All Holy reached into the vehicle to pick up the coloured boxes decorated with raffia. He picked one box up and she another. It was the breeziest of claims, at least he thought it was, so he spoke it in a way that made it seem like it was air escaping from his mouth, the winds running across the limestone walls: You know, while you were on stage, your husband tried to touch you, and you shifted your body away from him.

She stood stoic. The box was still in her arms and the back hatch of the van was open. She put the box down and sat on the edge of the van. A breath escaped and her face contorted. Her spine arched and she looked up at her brother. As she spoke tears came out of her face. I have been trying so hard to not let anyone know. All Holy put the raffia-wrapped box down onto the pavement. He sat next to her, she hoped he wouldn't touch her. It's okay, he said, it was such a small gesture that no one noticed it, I promise. Her tears had wet the navy mascara and there was a dark stain running down her white skin. No one knows, fix your eyes and let's get these gifts and pretend we are all okay, all happy families.

In the car, Honoured had gone into a monologue about her husband and Resurrection had disappeared down the well of thought. She kept watch on the traffic. Out on the streets were young men and girls in their glamorous Adidas. Range Rovers sprinkled the street. Waiting on the side of the road was a woman who was crossing at the most dangerous part of Burwood Road. It was near the pub, where three streets converged and there were cars turning in multiple directions at any time. The woman didn't care, she had defiant short hair and was wearing old jeans with a navy satin going-out top and Merrell hiking shoes. The shoes looked like she was going bushwalking, the jeans looked grunge and the halter gave an air of nonchalance. Resurrection stopped her van to let the woman pass and she breezed past them.

Honoured said she thought it was nice that she had let the woman cross and then said her father never let anyone cross, that he was selfish in his Kingswood. Resurrection turned to face her mother. She saw the breathlessness, a body heaving up and down, the repeated song, a familiar chorus—and she was fed up. Then leave! For a while Honoured kept talking, not listening to what her daughter had said. And when she realised, she stopped, mimicked her daughter's voice, and said, Leave him! Leave him? Listen to the stupid things you say, when all I want to do is talk. Resurrection drove to the top end of the street where a red light caught them and they were forced to halt on top of the bridge of the train station.

It was late afternoon, and the sun was encroaching on the horizon. Just out the front of the train station, some youths crossed in front of them, they wore all their best clothes at once.

The boys in shirts that showed too much skin and the young women in heels that would have to be taken off after too many RTDs when they knew they wouldn't be able to dance anymore. She looked at all of them, could see them in their too-shiny cheap Shein clothes. And realised she had never been like them. Never been reckless enough to try and wear heels the whole night while going out on the town, never even really went clubbing. She saw the girls' mouths open in laughs and wished the young women love, a future and a sparkling world to roll out in front of them.

For so long, this train station had been the route to a manifested life. After primary school had ended, she had done one of those tests to get into a better school and was funnelled straight out of the local public system, to what the community called the 'private school run by the government'. Oh, how they had all been proud of her! How everyone in the community had shared their joy! Over six years for five days a week she had walked to this train station. From the ages of thirteen to eighteen there had been different incarnations of the same brown uniform that all the students at Sydney Girls High School were supposed to wear. The shit-brown tunic with mandatory stockings. One year black Mary Janes and another year Dr Martens. Sometimes sneaking in Blundstone boots if she could. Too much time cross-legged in libraries and study rooms, girls sitting down in front of piles of books was something normal. No one there ridiculed for wearing glasses or for carrying a book bag that was too heavy. When an assessment or test was handed back, each girl would look at their own results and then suspiciously to the side to see what the other girl had got. Shoulders would go up or hunch over at the results.

In art class, her pictures represented the feelings and character of her subjects. She had hands like her father's that were capable of graphic rendering down to the millimetre. She sketched her friends, using cross-hatching techniques and colours around them to indicate their personality types. A bit of a blue halo for the Isobel portrait (who was icy cool in her emotions) and explosions of red for Mandy (who blew up quickly since her parents' divorce). From her mother's side, she got a love of arithmetic and language. At her advanced school she got into the top class for mathematics. She sat close so she could hear the teacher and always had pen markings all over her textbooks. They didn't have Greek or Ancient Greek, but there was Latin from the remnants of an Anglo education establishment. She took it and did Greek on the weekends. She would take a train to go to Greek school in Bankstown, and in the final year she had been ranked third in the state. She excelled in Latin, although at times it was like being in a cheesy coming-of-age novel—Looking for Resurrection—competing with all the private schools and walking through their cloisters and into their million-dollar grounds. She would meet the private school kids and introduce herself. The boys wore shoes that were a bit too polished, and she would tell them about where she came from, about the train that ran through her backyard, and they would smile nicely at her, angle their heads down so they could look at her through the top of their glasses. At the Latin trials she would speak against these boys, whose yearly school fees cost more than the librarian's assistant salary that her mother earned. That this girl, who got welfare from the government to study, should compete against polished brogues and those of the yachting regatta, meant the world to her. And it had started right there at that train station in Belmore. Platform number one. 7.26 am. Express to Central.

It was that train that had taken her to the city, to her engineering degree at Sydney University, where not only was she the only person from a working-class suburb, but this time also the only girl. And she had been surrounded by people that she had never encountered before. Posh country boys who wore akubras. That rare and special child of migrants that grew up in Milsons Point, who claimed they were kin but to a point. Oh, how those rosy-cheeked boys in chinos and boat shoes, all with dull vacant stares, looked down on the girl still wearing her glasses and stockings. And she had to show them, with their trust funds and inheritance, that they were no match for her force. She had added a political economy degree to her electrical engineering one, did things they couldn't, showing them up for the lifeless blobs they were. She tried her hardest not to think of them, but the thoughts overtook her sometimes. Like when she had come home and realised that their coffee table was an old train window.

At Belmore train station she would cross the threshold to other lives. It was curiosity that got her on that train. She forced herself to knock on any door or walk down any hall, and most importantly to carry that curiosity into a form of freedom that allowed her to be in any room. Twenty-something years later, here she was again, waiting for the lights to go green, so that she could turn right and take her mother home. Her hard pursuit of success would have made any mother happy, but things didn't sit quite right with her own. If she was working at her job, Honoured would say that she should stay at home more with her children. Those children are without a despot! her mother would say. When she ran her three boys to three different football matches on the weekend, her mother would complain that she wasn't cleaning the house enough. No settlement, no peace between her and her mother. And as she turned right into the street past the community centre, her mother kept talking. She was telling her that she shouldn't have worn that internet bubble dress, that at her age it was time to be hiding her arms and not always have her tits out.

Her mother looked out at the modern blocks. She pointed over to the community hall as they passed. The last time she had been there was to vote, with her husband and grandchild. Their daughter knew that any outing in Belmore was a form of church, where they could show off to their enclosed community. The two old wogs, escorting their baby through the lines of people. She told her daughter that she had seen Mrs Dina from down the road. At the time Honoured had been with her third grandchild, who had the darkest of features and resembled them more than any other of their kin. But as proud as they were of this child, the fact that it was not to be baptised by them had caused them difficulties.

Resurrection had found out through her mother that her father didn't want to be seen in public with his grandchildren because they were Jews. He was embarrassed that his daughter had married a pagan. She had found out about this and been incensed, the white hotness becoming the familiar disappointment she had with her father. But things had changed. When her father noticed that the third one had his own storm-coloured eyes, his hard ideas melted. He found the logic to justify his emotions and spoke about it with his daughter. Weren't there all distinct kinds of Greeks? Didn't Thessaloniki have the highest number of Greek Jews? You know, they found shelter there during the Ottoman reign after their persecution from Europe? Wasn't there a part of Greece called Preveza where the Jews there spoke a hybrid Hebrew–Greek dialect? Didn't those Preveza Jews channel their history all the way back to an ancient boat that had capsized in the Ionian? She heard his stories that he gleaned from MySat and the shallowest of *Greek World* articles. But she knew his vanity had been turned by seeing a child that shared his eyes. That was all it had taken to undo it.

Resurrection held the thought that the third one did not seem like the others. She had read once about Hemingway seeing the Greek refugees of Asia Minor. Hemingway said that they had the quick darting eyes of a Greek, an alertness, although many couldn't speak the language. And when Resurrection had picked up the third as a baby, she saw his eyes looking at her and looking at the air, and she recognised this quality in him. He also had that link to his grandparents. Others saw him as a cruel and violent child, but Papou saw him as mischievous. The grandfather of the family quickly claimed the third as one of his own. No longer scared to be seen in public with his descendants, regardless of how pagan they were.

Her mother spoke about her favourite memory there: That's when Channel Two saw us pushing the third one when we were going to vote! Later that night all the Greeks called, telling us we were on the television! Pride swelled in her mother. Although she hadn't been lucky enough to take their children to communion, it was a consolation, a stroke to her pride, that she had been seen so publicly, by all their community, being caregivers to their grandchildren. In Honoured's mind, this public display of their grandparental duties was a redemption.

She kept driving, the thoughts like a flash flood. She remembered a story that had kept doing the family rounds. Her mother had taken baby number three to show him off to her friends at church. She was in the forecourt when a busybody they knew beelined for them. Busybody had her hair up in a bun and asked if it was time for that child to take the red wine and bread of Holy Communion. All of Honoured's friends looked at her, waiting for her response. They knew the secret and what the response would be. So when Honoured said, Oh, we have already given the child two communions this week, we wouldn't want to get him drunk, they had all laughed, and Busybody Bun asked what was funny. A drunk child! At the church!

That's what's funny. Oh no, said Busybody Bun, the Holy Spirit would intercede in the child's body and never allow anything like that to ever happen.

When Honoured's friends had told the story of her mother lying, right there in front of the shell that housed God and his people, the story became myth. Family friends repeated it with a winking nod. Honoured might lie in front of the church, but she would never transgress the rules of giving communion from the chalice to one that had not been dunked in the ceremonious brass baptismal font (even if the one was her own kin). It made a name for her. The kind of character she was, and at her core, it spoke to the woman she was. When this story was recounted to Resurrection, a shot of pride swelled over her, knowing that her mother was the kind of woman who held her beliefs sacred, but still managed to juggle the pressures of holding a grandchild and wouldn't think twice of protecting her own little Jew against the evil forces of Busybody Bun and the same gossips who tut-tutted the family for their pagan connection.

Resurrection had made her own life. It had started back at the train station, or it had begun earlier on the streets walking away from home, or in her bedroom when she had rolled up her brown stockings that was part of a uniform. She could have kept moving up, moved up and into another world, but she had decided to stay. She was the only person that could have moved away from the area, into a more aspirational one with better schools—but didn't. She wasn't like Christina Chrisoula, who had got that job in the city and immediately moved to

Double Bay, to look over Sydney, a newly adopted posh accent coming out of her mouth. She wasn't like Vasilis—now Basil—who ran a pioneering real estate agency that developed poor areas, but who made sure to live on the rich side of Sydney. She had stayed put. Bought a house locally, lived close to her mother to give her children an intergenerational experience and her mother something to do around retirement. She had made sure that her children had a public education—no child of hers would go to a private, international, or Catholic school. There was a series of values she lived by, and she made sure that one of them was being there for her mother. One of the most vulnerable women she knew. And as she drove her down this road, she realised that in living her mother's life and a life for her mother, she wasn't living her own life. It came out in her driving. A slight swerve over the middle of the road, a correction, and she had agency again.

When they drove past the community hall, Honoured asked her daughter what had happened to her dream of helping people in politics. As an overachieving teen, Resurrection had participated in the community youth group. She had been cited for greatness and was immediately called The Chairperson. When all the girls in her school had had a half-up, half-down hairstyle, she had worn the tightest ponytail. When pants and skirts had been at the height of a Drew Barrymore nineties fashion, she had worn tight black jeans as a nod to their efficiency. Chairperson Resurrection meant to help people; this had been her central interest in politics. And now when help was needed, like her son needing guidance through a school struggle or her mother needing to go to physio, she was there, sandwiched between both. As she reflected upon her dreams of going into politics, she looked to her side, saw her mother had her specialised cane lying on her lap. Behind her, on the back seat, were footballs and dirty shoes wrapped in plastic bags. One of the kids had left a sandwich bag in the car, and the product inside had started to crust over with edges of deep green fuzz.

She answered with a sigh. The road unfolded beyond them, and Resurrection turned on the radio that had been set to Classic FM. Max Richter's interpretation of Vivaldi's 'Autumn' started to play throughout the cabin of the car. Her mother changed the subject and asked her daughter why she had gone this way to the family home, and Resurrection said she wanted to go a different way.

Through a few lanes and past some other things was the great All Saints Church of Belmore. The family had grown up in walking distance of the church. During the Holy Week when Greeks were asked to prepare themselves for the resurrection of Jesus, their house became a central point for cousins who drove in, found a park, and then walked together to go to the church. Part of the ritual during Holy Week was to abstain from all animal products including oils and sugars. On Holy Friday, when no work could be done with nails and hammers or needles and the house must be free of the joyous sounds of music and television, the extended family would all gather. And it was suspiciously joyful, the families of the three sisters in Australia together, all dressed up, in their nice clothes for God. Gathering to walk to a church, convenient but also replicating the village life and what their ancestors had done years before them. Those mountain Greeks, with their limestone skin and their pine-smelling hair.

There had been growth since their forty years in the area. Houses had become nicer, trees thicker, and prices had started to go up. Bungalows had lost their columns for rendered brick posts and lemon trees had been removed from yards to make way for undesigned gardens full of native shrubbery and flora that would attract back the old cockatoos and delicately coloured rosellas. But also, the church kept on buying the land around it. It started with one house and each time another one was for sale, the Archdiocese would buy it up. Eventually they had bought up enough land for a block and were still going. The Archies had a big plan to create a Greek private school for all the descendants of their community, where it was designated that their children would be lucky enough to go. They had found a pre-eminent architect of the community, internationally award-winning, who had worked with some of the great modernists, and got him to design the concrete and wood creations of the school. Reflected daylight was bounced into the classrooms, using angled coloured blade walls. No such luck or light or architecturally designed spaces for Resurrection and her peers when they had gone to Greek school. Underneath the great domes that made up the church was a basement with a hall, alongside the hall were classrooms which closed with accordion doors. It was there she had gone to Greek school when she was in primary school and got the classical education of Religion, Language, History and Ancient History. It was down in the bowels of the church that her mother had made an extra income by being one of the teachers of the community. Eventually her daughter was in the class, and once when her mother lost control of the class, she slapped her own child to make a point to the others. It worked—she never lost control of the class again.

The church had changed with the ambitions of the community. In turn, the buildings reflected this. Were the Gucci Greeks a direct response to this? Resurrection wondered. Did the postmodern architecture scatter the too common Louis Vuitton insignia amongst the community? She drove further down the street and her mother pointed to the lemon tree of a family that lived near the church. Remember when your brother complimented that lemon tree and the next day she came over and gave us all her lemons? Resurrection remembered that lemon woman and the generous gesture. She reflected on all these old Greeks, who practised their old pastoral ways, and she smiled at the generosity of the woman who had given all those yellow globes to her family, all that while ago, after—pop—a simple compliment from a family member. Their old village life and the values they had as land-owning peasants still defined them. Half a world away the Greeks of the diaspora still gave each other their bountiful harvests of golden lemons in plastic Coles bags and homemade pressed olive oil in two-litre Coke bottles. The cycle went over and over here. Generational circadian rhythms: families grew and changed, and this had been the experience for Resurrection. As her children had grown, as she had wanted more from life, the goddess in her had grown. Agrarian, Anatolian, Arcadian—this goddess was not enough. They passed the church and her mother did the intuitive gesture of crossing herself three times, a demand one must do if born into the faith.

That lemon giver was a nice lady, her mother mumbled, that woman was nice, but oh the things that her family put her through, she said. Her mum whispered the words 'husband' and 'gambler' in Greek. Each syllable of the whisper tore at the cabin of the car. Her daughter asked why she was whispering when there was no possible way of anyone hearing them. I whisper because of the gravity of it all, said her mother. I whisper for us, not for them. It was the flippant poetry of her mother, her natural rhythms for emotions of language, that always wrenched her daughter's heart, to the point where her life had coalesced around the feelings of her mother.

The mudflow of all these feelings was too much. They approached the newly built roundabout at the intersection. The traffic ahead of them started slowing down. She saw that the house her friend had grown up in had a sold sign in front of it. On the footpath there was a young man in vintage rollerskates pushing himself through the world. An electrical box painted in an army green stood out to them. She remembered the way it had hummed as she passed it going to the church. The humming of electricity filled her with a longing for the past, to go back and tell the little one, the version of her she could see, that the things that were going on, that the violence in the house would make her look too much at her books, too much at what others needed her to be and that her sense of self would be so entwined with her mother—that instead of becoming an electrical engineer, or a political economist, she would spend a life advocating for working people in unions and legally advocating for women in abusive relationships. She couldn't hear the electricity, but it was a whisper, and it followed her low, low, low, to the roundabout, and there she stopped the car, let some drivers pass, and then said, Fuck it. Driving over the roundabout, cars stopping to beep her, going over it like a speed hump. Her mother laughing, Well that was fun.

They drove onto the street that her mother lived on. When she had lived there, it had all been brown brick postwar bungalows that occupied quarter-acre blocks, which the families then built into double-storey houses or turned into cheap duplexes that were bought and then sold for a higher price. The greenery had become better too. Red bottlebrushes were thicker and grew taller. They had to be pruned around the hanging electrical wires and the trees made a U-shape, the grey branches open, like welcoming arms. She pulled into her mother's extra-long driveway and Honoured asked her to stop, she didn't want to be a bother and get her daughter to drive all the way up to the house. Resurrection glanced over the complicated four-pronged walking stick, rolled her eyes to herself and put on a sweet milk-pie voice that said, It's okay, I'm happy to drive you all the way to the house. Mum Van approached the house and drove over the lawn. From the large front-facing windows, she saw the blind pull back and her father peering out to see what had woken him from his afternoon siesta. Her ring finger intuitively pushed down the button of the driver's window. She looked up again and her father was descending the stairs in front of the house. Her mother, next to her, pleaded that she be nice to him. And then there he was, slightly groggy from his nap, but excited to see his daughter, she saw him wide-eyed, anticipating saying something to her, the words ready to explode with enthusiasm out of his mouth. She was greeted with a Hello, Girl! You look-a-the nice today! She didn't acknowledge the compliment, looked at him through her glasses and asked, What is more important than seeing your grandchildren on their big day? She knew the answer, that he had had a decade-long feud with members of the family and their fights were older than earth, than dirt, than rocks. And what could she speak to? For they had lived through a civil war and tried to survive relative killing relative and this meant that—oh yes—could they ever hold grudges. Even as recently as last year at an acquaintance's funeral, his wife's sister and her husband had tried to make overtures. They were grieving, wearing their blacks, and her father had stood there, stoic in a suit, pretending that no one had said hi to him.

There is something I need you to do about the house, he said to her. This one looks fine, you don't need to do anything about it. Not this, he said. Do you mean your house in Greece? she said. He had energy to expel but her mother was trying to get out of the van. He had the capacity to monologue at any time, in anyone's time of need, in a singsong voice that sounded charismatic, but really, he spoke with the timbres and tones of a man who tried to lure anyone into themselves by using their pain. At her side, she saw that her mother had grabbed the handle above the door and was holding on to the armrest. Honoured tried to manoeuvre her body at an angle so she could pivot out of the passenger seat. Resurrection turned the engine off, put the handbrake up and jumped out of the car to go and help her mother. Her father followed her around the car. He was wearing old blue canvas pants that had been burned by the flailing sparks of metalwork flames. He had sewn pockets on them, the seam looking like an industrial craft stitch that one would see on a leather recliner or the inside of a bag. His daughter looked him up and down curiously. There was something embarrassing about his homemade stiches, there was something endearing about them too. The stitch and pattern seemed capable, technically correct, but also too obvious. She reached over to her mother and her mother pushed her away, claiming she didn't need any help. I'm fine! she wheezed with effort. She stayed there, one arm on the open door, another arm on the roof of the car, ready to hold her mother straight if she fell. Honoured pretended her daughter wasn't helping her but leaned on her as each bung leg came out of the car. Resurrection knew she wasn't allowed to help her mother, despite it being easier and saving all the time in the world. She knew she had to pretend that she just happened to be standing there, this charade of helping but not outwardly helping to save face and create dignity.

She felt the heft of her mother on her body, pressed up against the bubble dress. Her father was on the other side, he pulled out an envelope from one of the hand-stitched pockets and then a piece of paper from the envelope. He unfolded the piece of paper and thrust it towards her. The heft of her mother meant that she had to reorientate her feet to take some of the weight, and she thanked her life that she had been doing reformer Pilates for the longest of times, her muscles long and lean and her core strength able to take almost double her weight.

She looked at the letter. It was in Greek and on the top right corner she recognised the seal as the symbol for the municipality of the Lefkada. Unlike her mother, her father had come from a seaside village, which gave hints as to why his family was so strange. Historically, those who dwelled seaside had strange mariners come in and out of their ports; this meant that their personalities hardened, and they engaged with outsiders but with a veneer of superficiality. His village on the edge of town had been exposed to the elements, wind so hard that it eventually became a windsurfing destination. But the wind beat the people in it, and sometimes the fish hauls never arrived. His family mythology also included a story about a great-aunt who was kidnapped by pirates and never returned. All these elements—dependence on government, a sneaky but mercantile engagement—made the people align with the fascist tendencies of hierarchies, religion, and monarchy. All things that were against her value system. Each visit to that place reminded her. She hated it. Resurrection had seen the seal the last time she had been in Greece.

About one year ago, Resurrection and her mother had been leaving the council prefecture of her father's village. After hours of negotiating with the bureaucrats, they had lodged the updated forms for the house. These forms had been sent back and forth between Greece and Australia. It was the one thing they had to do on that side of the island. She was free of the children, they were on the other side, playing with their cousins, unsupervised in the way that they could be when they were not in Sydney. She had walked out of the government building with her mother and down its steps to the bay side. Her mother took one step at a time, but the stairs that were made from rocks did not have any purchase. The heel of her mother could not find itself. The rocks in that part of the town were unwelcoming and decided to let her slide. Her mother's body leaned diagonally, unsteady, and then rolled back, her body falling backwards, her arms reaching out to find something to hold on to. And when her hands knew they weren't going to find anything, she waved them around, like she was flying, as if she could ascend. It made the crash on the ground teeter on comic. But she landed on her side, and as Resurrection processed the movements, her mother's face carved out an emotion upon it. The brows leaned into a pain just as the eyes turned from muddy brown wells to glass pools. Behind the eyes expanded a great vastness, all the way through a terrain that ended up as sadness. Her daughter saw beyond the physical pain.

Her mother sat there alone, on her bum, both legs extended outwards. Something had been too familiar. Her position sitting there looked so profoundly sad that it had welled up Resurrection's sympathy, devouring her own self. Her sadness overflowed; her own eyes felt the sting of the salt air. When she looked over, she didn't see her mother there. What she saw was a little girl in pain. She saw the middle daughter who had been overlooked and made sacrifice for a boy. A little girl limping. A four-year-old waiting in a hospital ward for a year.

She had seen in the girlhood photos of her mother and her sisters that there was playfulness in the others but not in her mother. All her life she'd known her seriousness, her stern face, the adult scowling woman. She thought Honoured born an adult. A cynical chain-smoker. And when her daughter had seen her there, her mother transforming into a child right in front of her, it engulfed her heart too much. And there in her father's village, Resurrection became welded to Honoured.

She had searched for her phone to call an ambulance but remembered she was in Greece. She flagged down some pedestrians and then ran back into the building to get more help. Many hands lifting her mother into the car. In the back seat, her mother wept all the way to the main hospital on the other side of the island. They pulled up in the emergency bay and were greeted by sixteen family members. All of whom had stopped what they were doing after a chain SMS was sent all the way through the family. Every single descendant of Torch and Spirit Peasant on that island had gathered at the hospital. They asked what was wrong and if they could donate blood.

Resurrection was too close to those memories. Things were coming through now. The rising waters became regrets. Doubt about taking her mother to that place. Doubt about taking her mother to Greece. Doubt about driving her mother. This slightest crack, knickpoint in the bedrock, had created a fissure in the self and she did everything she could to get back quick smart in the van and on her way home. She told her father she would look at the documents another time.

Her mother took each foot slowly up the stairs. She yelled out to her daughter one final instruction. Do not forget what I told you. You are losing too much weight! You look like a scarecrow! Resurrection started the car and put up the window.

While she was driving home, she started to read signs. Down the driveway and up the street, the bottlebrushes were waving her away. Over the roundabout she went back past the buzzing electrical box, it was still military green, and she remembered its sound like a warning. And as a girl, walking to Greek school alone, she remembered the loneliness she had created in herself, at odds with the landscape around her. She went past the Greek church, the night school she came to as a youth, the place she got slapped as a teenager. Its dome above seemed impenetrable and unaccepting. The change had taken her memories and she was glad. Past the community centre and her aspirations, now it was a place where groups held daggy dances. It was locked up tight, bars on its windows. And its hard bricks made it look more like a detention centre than a community hall. She drove over the bridge where the train station was. She imagined the commuters underneath, coming on and off the platforms, as they had done their whole lives and as she had done her whole life. Police officers with sniffer dogs checked every passenger. Past the cake shop she licked her lips, thinking about their almond cookies, but did not want to go in, the men outside a bulwark. And just as she got home the caterers were pulling out of her driveway.

She put her van in its spot. As she got out, she could see her eldest boy in the computer room through the window. In the front yard her husband was smoking a cigarette with her brother.

PART 7

2022

CANTERBURY HOSPITAL
ALL HOLY CITIZEN

Do you know what? Last night I worked till 2 am earning minimum wage. I put a suburban and Coke on the counter of the bar and copped a perve at a gay guy's chest through his open shirt. In between his pec line was a gold medallion of Medusa's angry face and snake hair. She tried to turn me to stone, but I'm used to your death stares and my real icon is Medea. You know this. My friends too. Even Lemon Tree has scolded me: Stop being so obsessed with Medea! But I adore her. I love her unhinged at the break-up of her relationship and then her transformation in the second act into the terrifying producer of her own drama. Sometimes I imagine you as Medea. I have in the past. The character comes from Colchis which is modern-day Georgia. It is a country of the Caucasus (Caucasians, lo!) and the people there have your colouring. In your late twenties you had black hair down to your waist. I've seen the photos with your trademark lack of vanity. You inherited pale white skin from your Vlach heritage. Australians, who are notoriously bad at guessing people's heritage, could never clock you. You were such a witchy barbarian. Men would stop you in the street—Excuse me, are you Indian? Excuse me, are you Irish?—and your eyes would fix forward as you walked away furiously, a cape of black hair trailing behind you. Like most gays, I can't resist a furious woman. Did you know that?

When I saw the back of the last customer, limping out of the place with her empty pockets inside out, all dollars lost on the pokies, I closed and cleaned the bar. It was about 1 am. Just the sounds of pokies and re-runs of football matches on the television and a song about thieves wailing through the radio, the tinny sound from the speakers competing with my pattering feet as I ran around the bar. I put each glass away and polished a tray of wineglasses, removing lipstick from the rim. I named the colours. Burned Limestone. Fuchsia Loquat. Cherry Earth. When the schooners and midis had been piled away, I poured industrial bleach on the tiles, pumping it out of a five-litre white plastic container. The yellow label wrapped around it named it a category-four chlorinated floor cleaner. I love the order of cleaning signs, clear instructions, sans serif fonts. It's the Order of Things that gets me. It orders my mind. I held a wooden broom with polyurethane bristles, I scrubbed the gel into the broken tiles. Wished I could cut the dowel in half, easier to hold with one hand. The fumes rose to my nose and made me dizzy. Spinning into a fugue state. Maybe I was the oracle. I took a breath and looked up to the ceiling, I saw its grey fibreboard and fluorescent lights of boredom. Institutional. Unglamorous. Why have hospital lighting in a bar? With a stream of water out of a hose, everything ran off down a drain. I walked around the bar, my foot almost slipping on what felt like moss-covered rocks. It felt like the wet earth of a forest path. As I heard the water running down, I told myself, I am going to clean my house like this! I want to clean the house the way you cleaned our house. Everything so bright with pride. But I got to my rental apartment late, the place was a mess and I decided to clean the following day. I took off my work polo and rayon pants right in the living room. I went to limp into the kitchen, and I ended up falling asleep on the floor.

Baba woke me with a call at 2.30 am. It was unusual. I reached over and picked up the phone. When I answered it, there was silence. He repeated my name in a question. There were loud spaces in between each time he called my name, it made the voice sound like it was coming from another dimension. He said there was something wrong with you, that I should see you. And because he never calls me, I knew something was up. Needing to wake myself up, I went to the bathroom, splashed water on my face like he had taught me—he thinks it's a military trick to stay awake, but it's just a thing people do. The bathroom cabinet was open, fungal cream next to zinc cream. Bottles of serums and oils next to each other, manifesting my quest for Korean glass skin. Rose hip oil in a pink vial with a gold-rimmed edge, it looks too ornate to use, but it was given to me by a masc. I noticed more moles had appeared on my face. In Greek we call them the same word for olives. Every time I see them on my face or look down at them on my arms as I type, I think of them as the things that link me to the trees on our ancestral farms in Greece that are older than the nation of Australia. I love eating olives. They taste bitter. You know sometimes I say that it was my ancestor who became the first olive tree. She had a fight with a partner, fell asleep way after midnight and was so bitter that she turned into the tree that bore the bitter fruit.

I drove to your home through the night. I stopped off at 7-Eleven, parked in a spot near the door. Inside I headed straight to the coffee machine. I put a paper cup under the silver spout and pressed the one-dollar latte option. It poured, I paid, I sipped and I was more awake. Back on the road, it was full of people going home from the city. The party kids in their WRXs, their cars ready to transform into robots (probably Autobots), and engines that grimaced with illegal mufflers. I saw bandits and brigands on dirt bikes riding in packs. When they spotted police officers, they drove off-road and over the parks so they couldn't be followed. Feels like I'm never going to leave Western Sydney. After Belmore became gentrified, this place with its junkies and law-breaking youths feels like the familiar place I grew up in.

I was driving too recklessly for you. Switching lanes while switching radio stations. AM was mundane with its Anglo monotone; FM was too nervous with its bad pop hooks. On community radio there was a religious service. It was a prosperity preacher. He told me God wanted me to be rich but

I didn't believe him. Do you remember the first time I asked you if God existed? I was so young that I had to look up at you while you were sitting at the kitchen table. There was a hand-loomed tablecloth on it, gold thread in the shape of diamonds. In time I would recognise it as the handicraft of your ancestral island but way before that my insufferable gay pretensions and aspirations would make me think of this stuff as 'tacky' and 'very un-Bauhaus'. The hand-loomed tablecloth was plastic-covered, making it shine, emphasising the crystal bowl with fruit. You were smoking Winfield Blues, having graduated from Holiday Menthols. My cigarette queen, a plume of smoke around your head. Your hair was short, a black bob, and you exhaled smoke through the side of your mouth. You said: I cannot tell you if God exists, no one can and if they do, they are lying.

As I drove a space opened up in between two Mack trucks and I sped through them. The air-conditioning hiss stopped being comforting, it became claustrophobic. More time on the road and soon I was driving down the long driveway to your house. The front yard. Days of heat and rain had caused the grass to grow knee-high. Food plants were rampant, parsley and rocket clumped under trees. The night creates shadows for many things to hide in. This time I wasn't scared because I was scared for you. The olive tree that our white goat Afroditi used to climb was thinner than I had remembered. Baba had been pruning. There was an Aleppo pine that Baba had smuggled illegally into Australia. It transferred me back to the Greek island. There were no drunken Anglos spewing in this bronze landscape, no rocky Mykonos beaches that smelled like amyl. I think a Greek island should consist of a pro-junta village hugging the coast and a communist one hidden in the mountains. One of them is yours and one of them is Baba's.

You were facedown on the mattress when I walked into your bedroom. It was a play-by-play repeat of 2017. Baba was in front of the TV, watching ERT and complaining about Syriza. Bloody new lefties and so forth. Next to you I saw a bucket that held some meagre spew. On your bedside table there was a wheat cracker, a whole bite taken out. The sheets covered some of your body but your leg was exposed. The one that has all your childhood damage. It was red and swollen. The skin had started to flake, and I put my hand on it. It was the devil's temperature. I went to the side of the bed to speak to you. I crouched near your face. Your eyes were colourless, your cheeks squished around your mouth and messy grey hairs were stuck to your forehead. I asked if you were okay, but you said you needed sleep. And I saw that your lids kept falling, that your will couldn't control them. You said there was nothing wrong with you, but I have ears and eyes, and my hands that touched your body knew you were too hot. So I called the ambulance and they only sent the patient transport. It made the whole thing slightly less dramatic as you waited facedown on your mattress.

You were still in your bed when the two paramedics inserted the fluid into your arm. You immediately came back. Your eyes opened. You were more than lucid; you were back to being bitter and generous. You said something about me to the paramedics—ignore my son—and then you offered the paramedics gifts of Ferrero Rocher for doing their job. I wasn't embarrassed by your generosity or my public dismissal. I was just embarrassed to be around the paramedics. They had utilitarian healthy bodies. Both were blond. And they had teeth that gleamed. People whose parents had spent money on braces and were taught how to regulate their emotions without drugs. My lack of health was visible in my hunched body. My poverty visible in my clothes. My poor smell. The only way I resembled the Ancients was in smell. I looked into their eyes to see if they saw me the way I felt. I could not see. They got you out of the house and moved you to the hospital. I was ashamed that I could not do more. As an afterthought they told me to follow. And just before you left, I told you not to die, otherwise I would go to the funeral dressed as you. You laughed and I thought this time you would be okay. I said this to you in Greek and the paramedics looked at me confused, like I was talking about them. It made me think about how you spoke your own language around everyone. And the strangers that told you to shut up. And how I never understood why I could say fuck you without consequence, but shut up would get a belting, things thrown at my head, solids or fluids.

At 4 am I drove down the ramp into the Canterbury Hospital car park. My Suzuki stopped at an automated gate directly under the Community Health Unit and I put the gear in neutral. This part of the hospital was as familiar to me as the smell of bleach. You remember my twenties when I went through psychosis.

Resurrection doesn't remember. I've asked her. She has tried to block it out, but I know you still take it with you. I often wonder how the things I went through compounded the problems you had. Are they hidden in your body parts? At the boom gate a robot authoritarian voice told me to take the ticket that it spat out. It was hard paper and snapped from the machine. I turned the steering wheel right, put the gear into first and moved my body forward. When I drive in enclosed spaces it makes me feel like I need an intimacy with the windscreen. I drove past all the parking spots reserved for the doctors and nurses. Next to them was the elevator that went directly up to the Community Health Unit. When I used to have my annual meetings with doctors, I would take this elevator. It fits only two people and goes to two spots: the car park and the reception—which it opens straight into. When I used to get out of the elevator, I would inform a nurse behind the scratched perspex glass that I had an appointment and wait on a row of linked plastic chairs. I would sit there and contemplate the patterned leaflets in different community languages. I would look at the perspex and hope that I had never contributed to the scratches. After being let through the security doors, I would meet with psychologists and psychiatrists. They would put me on various kinds of medication, some that worked and some that didn't. Every time I go into this hospital car park, some old memory comes up and I find a new detail about it. Driving through this time, I became sleepy again, the lids of my eyes wanted to fall and I thought about the different kinds of pills that I had swallowed for seven years. The pale blue ones called Abilify that came out of a bottle, the green ones called Risperdal, and then the white ones called Solian that came out of blister packs. After taking the green ones twice for two separate experiences, they stopped making them because they gave patients heart defects. You always insisted I take those drugs. Made me open my mouth and put them in. Swallowing water after to check if I had done it right. I feel like I lost a decade of my life to psychosis. A decade of my life driving up and down ramps, trying to get better health outcomes.

Do you remember once I was driving you to physical therapy and you were in the passenger seat? We were looking out the front windscreen when the car rolled to a stop. At the pedestrian crossing, a woman in torn jeans pushed a Bugaboo pram over the zebra stripes. You always had an I Need to Say Something energy—an I Should Be Able to Talk Too spirit. Your language flows, something inside you needs to be expunged. You were reflecting on your recent time in Greece. You had seen so many single mothers. You pointed it out like it was a new phenom-enon. I pointed a finger to the sky. Actually, Mama! Divorce is common in present-day Greece! Greeks changed with the times, unlike here, where the peasants froze! You didn't handle it; you gave it back. You said to me that you weren't scared of what the community thought of you. Those people? Most of the people in our community, some of your best friends were nothing better than goat herders! That came out with a laugh. Then you said to me that the reason you never got divorced was because you were scared that my father would take his double-barrelled shotgun and shoot me and my sister. The car stopped. The road in front of us was empty. The cabin became small, and my face got closer to the windscreen. You were looking outside the passenger window. I could only see the back of your head, a helmet of grey hair. You let out the tiniest snort, followed by a laugh that was so dismissive that it could have crushed marble. As if to say, how stupid and naive I had been all this time. But I knew, because I have always had this fear in me. Since I was a child I have remembered that I have been scared. It has resulted in so many sleepless nights.

You tried so much to help me sleep. You used to sit on the side of my bed and tell me myths. Your sleeping attire was an oversized t-shirt with a frayed hem. Its neckline had warped and it exposed your milk-white collarbones. I remember your column of long black shiny hair. I thought the white skin and glossy hair were supernatural. Strands of black hair would fall upon me as you tucked me under a green and gold doona that had a picture of a boxing kangaroo on it. I would hold you ransom until you told me stories of Hercules and his Twelve Labours. I remember him killing the lion with the gold fur and saying to myself—There! There he is!—as I saw him run across the plane of your thigh. The black hairs on your leg were stones. The hollowed flesh from your childhood wounds was the valley he hiked through. I'd fall asleep to the rhythm of your voice.

One time you couldn't be bothered with the stories. I was lying in bed, sleepless, and a feeling of fear climbed into me. The bedside lamp was on, and I was shaking. My breath was shallow.

I hopped out of bed, got on all fours, and peered behind the dust ruffle to see if anyone was under there. You heard me go bump when I landed on the carpet. From the other room you yelled, Go back to bed! Turn off the lamp! I did. The moonlight made shadows in the room, and I double-checked each one. Outside I heard a rustle amongst the grapevines and it stopped me from sleeping. For the whole night I waited and looked for monsters. I didn't sleep at all. And sometimes I still don't. Expecting men or monsters to get me, those stories you told me were a distraction. I still find myself being bothered by this all.

There were the men that scared me and the ones that I thought would make me heal. One of the psychiatrists that gave me the pills was someone I was drawn to. I called him Dr Silverbeard. He was in his fifties. He had receded grey hair and a full beard. He wore glasses and his thick lips muffled his voice. He had a South American accent, and his voice came out like comforting fried food. If I had a libido back then, my skin would have become flushed; my parts would have moved in his presence. But that description is too cheap a way to describe how I held my body still around him. Or how the lids of my eyes opened slightly more when I looked at him. Or how the small consult room was filled with too much brightness because my pupils had dilated. In his presence I turned my head to the side more, so my ears could take in his dulcet tones. I remember him looking at me, his eyes over the top of rimless rectangle glasses. I was to be assessed, a work object. I was part of his job and in our consultations, I never knew how to behave. Sometimes I'd straighten my back and put my shoulders down while trying to make references to my understanding of the way culturally and linguistically diverse communities experience a mental health crisis, because I wanted to show him I was intelligent and different from the other nutjobs he treated. He was stoic and responded by taking notes. My transference of healing projected right onto him, it was conditional to my experience, and I was like vulnerable people before, falling in love with someone more powerful. I made the mistake of desiring someone because they had control and information about myself. I thought him a healer, my affectations removed all fear. But I keep wondering if the person I feared was myself. The memory of Dr Silverbeard passed as I found the closest parking spot in the car park to the elevator.

This morning when I came to the hospital, I saw four cars parked in the area designated for the public. I hadn't expected that many at 4 am. All were huddled close to the elevator, the low concrete ceiling stretching out around them into the grey expanse, the white guiding lines lit by fluorescents. I parked my car, locked it up and checked my pockets for my keys and phone. It was just a few steps to the elevator and the metal doors parted when I arrived in front of them. Inside the elevator was a nurse wearing a flak jacket and she looked up at me, startled. She stepped out very slowly, her eyes forward. She was situationally aware of my presence, looking at me from the side of her eyes. Her keys were in her hand, I heard the metal jingle as her hand holding the keys turned into a ball, the keys sticking out from her knuckles, like small jagged bronze knives. She moved around me, no eye contact. You know what I'm wearing—black work pants, my shoes too scuffed with beer stains on them, my favourite Adidas tracksuit jacket that I purchased because it had a mixture of shapes on it, circles and three stripes that reminded me of some of the forms of the Russian painter Wassily Kandinsky. He was one of the early pioneers of abstract art, before the CIA used the movement as a form of soft cultural propaganda. He produced complex theories about shapes and colours, and when I saw some of the patterns on this Adidas jacket at Bankstown Foot Locker, I knew where the German designer of this garment had got their inspiration from, and it reminded me of my time at Sydney College of the Arts. I purchased it. But a night nurse, finishing an overworked shift, entering an empty car park at 4 am, didn't know this. I understood exactly what I looked like in my black tracksuit jacket, black pants, and messy beard. I still smelled of beer and it was morning.

The elevator rose with me in it. On the wall was a flyer for Lamaze classes near the maternity wards, it reminded me of when Resurrection had given birth. There was an A4 flyer for hydrotherapy classes in the hospital pool, this evoked the times that I had driven you to them. There were signs for maximum occupancy, but this elevator was massive. Big enough to roll two full beds into it. The doors opened on the level of the Acacia ward. When I exited, I grazed my fingertips on the threshold and tapped it three times. I'm superstitious. If I had time and the church had been open, I would have gone in there and lit a candle for you in the narthex. But I walked past the closed cafeteria, where inside I could see all the treats that I mindlessly craved. I saw plastic-wrapped lamingtons covered with a hard choc outer layer and gritty coconut flakes. I knew they were filled with a synthetic buttercream and yellow cake that had the texture of a dish sponge. Too much work, too much thinking, too many things up in the air and the lure of mindless eating was too much. I thought about how the rich would never understand this form of thinking, because they had parents who believed in self-esteem and therapy and healthy organic diets and not expressing emotions. I thought about how you mindlessly ate those sugary treats, despite your diabetes, cholesterol and swollen digits. I remembered how I kept using drugs, despite my penchant for psychosis, my multiple bouts of madness. Both of us wanted to be out of our bodies in separate ways. The rich will never understand. So fuck them. But today, even if the cafeteria had been open, I would still have passed it and headed to the ward to check up on you.

I walked down the hallway to the Acacia ward, it was long and on either side of it were windows that looked out over dimly lit rock gardens. The floors had been cleaned, and somewhere in the building I heard a linoleum buffing machine, its hum mixing with footsteps and beeps. My posture was so bad, chest over itself. A nurse in light blue scrubs was walking towards me. From the side of my eye, I could see he was swarthy. A flash of dark beard and hair. Even though it was the earliest of mornings and the sun was ready to crack open the day, I felt an intuitive shame about my appearance, the same appearance that had just scared a female nurse, the same appearance that still wanted to be desirable to a man. Despite that familiar embarrassment, I still managed to turn my head up and get a closer look at the man walking past me. His hair was hard with a shine. His shirt held onto his body straight and hugged against his flat stomach. He looked like a stereotypical Greek guy from the suburbs. I realised I knew him. His name was Lust. He was a guy who I had met when I worked at the local supermarket. Partly attracted to him because of his giant Greek hook nose and mostly attracted to him because he was there. There is a way circumstance, proximity and enclosed spaces can create links with beings when there are none, it's the way they get zoo animals to breed.

Once we had been out to a Greek nightclub. I remembered he wore a pastel blue satin shirt that was tight against his body. That night he kept looking for me and I kept dancing away. He liked punk bands, which I didn't find inconsistent with his love of Greek music, since both had ornate instrumentation and dedication to extreme emotions. He looked the same, hadn't aged in that way that most Greek men don't. Kept his lithe body and quick darting eyes. I nodded to him, and he looked at me—a stranger. The image that I held on to, when he walked past me, was of his eyes, they were onyx holes. One of his hands swayed, his palm flat, and the other hand was in his pocket, behind him was the window that looked out over the hospital rock garden, light chiaroscuro on the succulents and rounded pebbles.

When I reached the end of the hallway, my hand was in the pocket of my jacket, my fingers gripping hard around my wallet. The look askance from Lust rewound my life back years and stirred an inner reflection on who I had imagined I would become as a person, and how I had inevitably turned out. I felt a deep shame in myself, you saw this in me as well, this shame of my big ideas, you called them my megalomanias and philosophies. It made me reflect on two young men together, wanting each other but unsure of what to do.

I stopped at the entrance to the Acacia ward. I knew you were inside one of the rooms. I put my hand on the wall. Machines beeping like a symphony. The tear and pat of rubber-soled feet against the linoleum. A patient's cough. I turned around to see Lust one last time. My neck twisted; my hips followed. He was waiting for the elevator. His body was lean, his spine curved at the top, in the way of a tall person uncomfortable with their height. In the dark, in the institution, I saw him alone in a hallway. I reflected on being young and overconfident when I first met him. Back when I had met Lust, I had this sense that I was too good for the minimum wage work I was undertaking. That part of my queer limitless horizon was an infinity and a promise of potential that would take me away from the minimum wage and workplace uniforms and name badges. My vanity taught me I was better than earning under twenty dollars an hour for tasks that included helping customers find the right door lubricant or telling them we didn't have it. And I was carrying myself with a youthful arrogance, a contempt for the workplace.

This feeling of superiority—a temporary stopgap till the next best thing. This feeling that I was better than them for doing the same job. I was reminded of those thoughts as I looked at Lust in that hospital hallway. His presence was a reminder that my achievements had been thwarted, and ambitions scattered to that horizon. He had always been an afterthought. Like the jobs I held down, I didn't think much of the people that I met in those spaces. I'd wait for messages from someone else on my Ericsson Flip. There were others I thought more important. More worthy of my time. Like the politician I had slept with. Or the journalist I had slept with. Both were the kinds of men who would only see me privately, never in public. You saw my vanities and big ego. You called me out on it. Said that I couldn't have good politics if I treated those in front of me terribly.

Once I got messages from Lust telling me he'd come back from Greece. I didn't even know he had gone away. I was supposed to meet him in front of Stonewall bar, and I arrived late on a weekend. The line to get into the club was cut by a velvet rope alongside the footpath. The punters waited with folded arms and cigarettes in their mouths. Shiny shirts in emerald, amethyst, and pomegranate. Gay boys with frosted blond tips and white coral chokers. There were groups of men and single gay people and through the crowd I saw Lust sitting on the kerb. His head was so low, his shoulders and ears on the same imaginary line. He was a ball sitting on the kerb of Oxford Street and I looked around to see if I recognised anyone else, or to see someone that I could share with what I saw—a sad young man wearing his going-out jeans, sitting on a kerb, pretending it was a suitable place to rest. His shoulder was the closest thing to me, protruding, and my fingertips made their way there. There was a turn of his neck, his eyeball getting a sense of me. He smelled of aniseed liquor and L'Eau d'Issey. The crown of his head rolled back and forward. There was mumbling, so I shook him, trying to get him to speak more clearly. Behind us, men were laughing and carrying on, I had this immediate sense of being perceived, having an audience. That something was happening to me. He said he might have got AIDS on Mykonos and I asked what he meant, and he said he had only got head from a random on Elia Beach. He just looked at the ground, convincing himself of something untrue. He was out of his body and I squatted next to him, petting him with reassurance, telling him that oral sex couldn't do that. He shook his head, saying he had AIDS. And I asked again if he had had unprotected sex with anyone. I was straight down the line, asking him if he had used a condom and if it broke and he said no. Then I asked what he was worried about, but he shook his head and said, I've got it, I've got it, and from the lowest part of my stomach, a smile climbed its way out of me. The histrionics, the inability to deal with things, was familiar but I couldn't place it then, couldn't link the feeling of wanting to disconnect the body, turn the body into oblivion, through AIDS, through drugs, through too much sugar. Lust had a problem. It wasn't a desire for men or AIDS or the secrets from his family. His problem wasn't being a femme boy amongst the majorly masculine Earlwood Greeks.

Or partying to the worst Britney songs and going back to the NOFX posters on his bedroom wall. His problem was a familiar one of the poor: misdirection, worthy of sugary lamingtons or body-altering drugs, plain emotions put somewhere else. And I saw it visibly manifest in that hallway when I looked at him being a nurse. The way his spine curved, his shoulders hunched. When the elevator doors swung open, I saw him take one step towards it, his second step halfway to the elevator and that arched body following his too-long legs, the turn of his head to look back at me—confirmation that he had seen me and the mess of my uniform, my own tired stupor, my body leaning and crushing right into itself. The elevator doors closed and the hallway was void of people again. The linoleum on the floor. The stainless-steel railings that went across the walls. The downlights at night creating circles over the floor.

Just before I came into the ward to find you, seeing Lust made me remember the time you asked if I had AIDS. It was when I told you I was recovering from the flu, and I was sitting opposite you at the kitchen table. I could see your face through some garden-picked flowers that were in a crystal vase. I remember the way the smile spread across your face and your deadpan eyes. You couldn't get the terror of it. The spectre of it. The grim reaper mowing down people on screens. How I'm part of that in-between generation, too young to know too many people that had died of it, old enough to remember it becoming just a manageable thing. I still remember the stories of young healthy Greek and Italian boys coming back to their family members and then dying. Families telling the community it was just the flu. And you asked me if I had it, like it was air blowing in my face.

I know why you made that question tear at me. It was because I had written a letter to you and read it at an event called Men of Letters. I tried making a case that you are Medea. I presented all the cruel things that you said to me and my sister. Like when she took a big lawyer case to the High Court, and you dismissed her with a Pfft . . . will the High Court do the vacuuming? I told the audience details of your sorcerer ways, the reading of prophecy coffee cups, how the warble of a currawong meant death in the community. And the time you said, Of all creatures that can think and feel, we women are the worst treated things alive.

In the letter I recounted your history with Baba. How you had just got engaged to him and then decided to break it off. It was before me and my sister were born. He tried to win you back and wrote letters for a reconciliation. With the anger of the gods, he threatened to kill your young nieces and nephews. My voice had cracked on the stage when I read this. I told you about this. Afterwards people came up to me and congratulated me on my bravery. I was nervous from the attention, thinking about the way you had suffered for forty-something years, your shiny black hair turning a dull grey. My mouth broke into an uncontrollable smile. There was something perverse about my smile because there are no stage directions after catharsis, and I always thought you must smile when people congratulate you. And then I read that letter to you over the kitchen table. The one I read to the group of people. And between us, you were happy.

Because you wanted me to tell the world of this. You wanted sympathy for your plight, not only from me, but from an infinite number of anonymous strangers. But I know, even if that auditorium of people had lined up to wash your feet with their hair, it wouldn't be enough to prevent this time in the hospital.

I saw the entrance to the Acacia ward, there was a large desk. The desk was unstaffed but a whiteboard behind it listed the names of the patients and I saw our last name at the bottom of the board. Walking down the hallway reminded me of being in a hotel, looking at the numbers on the doors to find the right room. There were all kinds of people in each room. There were old wogs in some of the beds and young men in the others. Some of the curtains were pulled completely around, and where they were open, people slept or kept their eyes on a television that glowed a light over them. There was a young man in one of the beds. He had jet-black hair and smooth skin pulled over his high cheekbones; he was wearing a tight-fitting Adidas t-shirt and he looked at me with interest. There was a moment of self-awareness for him. He became aware of his own wide-eyed interest, looked back and away, like it was nothing. Maybe he had the same intentions as others who had given me that look. Maybe it was me mistaking the space for a hotel hallway, the young bed-bound man with his desire. Running into Lust had made me reflect on the waves that came to me in the hallway. I had a need to populate the hospital, its hallways and curtains, with memories of bodily interaction—the rubbing up of flesh and brains in a shared experience. Desire, wants and floods that made me alive and connect with what remained of my human experience. I saw that reluctant gaze of the young man in the hospital bed, and it reminded me of when I was on that Greek island that we come from.

It was the off-season on the ancestral island. I was in my thirties, and I remember thanking the sun god for the long hot days. Resurrection had brought the nephews to Greece and taken a flat near the main town. I wanted to be away from them, as close to the centre of town as possible. I stayed in a small hotel; it was empty apart from the room next to mine. During the mornings I'd ride a bike down to the water and sit on the pebble-covered beaches. For lunch I would eat frozen yoghurt and at night I'd go drinking at the bars, even though back then, recovering from psychosis, I was still a teetotaller. In the hotel I had been put next to the only other guests. She was a half-Palestinian, half-Greek girl, chubby and gregarious. He was one of those prized blond Greeks who worked on his family's olive grove. The girl had the prettiest dark features, her skin was bronze and her dark eyes were deep set in her head. The blond male shone for me at the time. I had the community in my head, the way those blond Greeks had such a choke on our imaginations. I assumed we had been put next to each other in the hotel to make it easier for the cleaners. At night when I couldn't fall asleep, I'd leave *30 Rock* on repeat on my laptop and let it run. Spent lots of time on the balcony. It looked over the old square, the restaurants whose tables sprawled across the old cobblestones. Places for tourists to eat. Every night I would look down on the tanned long Germans and Scandinavians. I'd check my GayRomeo site to hook up with men. The only men on the island that I got a response from were married men who I had a family connection with, so I avoided them. There were young hot proprietors of businesses, but those men had no interest in me, I was stung by rejection multiple times, and fair enough. The meds made me puffy, not just fat, but a permanent bloat. My skin had a yellow pallor, there were dark circles around my eyes. Apart from the bloat, the meds still made my arousals short or infrequent. My body wasn't used to the weight either, so my knees bent inwards, and I had a stiff gait that I had yet to fix. That was no way to greet the ancestors, no way to have a holiday, and instead of accepting my body, I kept trying to escape it. I rolled cigarettes, Port Royal that I bought duty free in Australia. I stayed on the balcony, sometimes sitting behind the fencing so no one could see me.

One night the Greek blond was on his balcony. When I went outside to smoke, I saw him standing there. To look at him was as easy as semolina custard. I was taken with his blond hair that had grown inches too long. It was tousled with grease and the strands fell over his forehead. His trimmed mutton-chops reached down to his jawline. He was the same height as me and looked half my weight. He had tanned skin that never went red. I watched him lean over his balcony, I lit a cigarette and waved my hand at him. We both stood there silently, on balconies next to each other. I had my body half over the railing and focused on the tourists and diners down below on the plaza.

After imagining my life differently, the cigarette in my hand was ending and I was getting to its filter. My thumb and forefinger held the base of the cigarette, squishing the bud together. His cigarette ended, I turned to look at him, my eyes hitting the side of his face. He asked me to roll one of mine and I did, offering to throw it over to his balcony, but he said that he would love to come over. A few seconds later he knocked on my door, I opened it. He entered the space and turned around to look at me. I gestured to the balcony and we both walked outside. There was no talking. I handed him what I had rolled, there was a slight surprise in his eyes that I had hand-rolled my own. My Greek, spoken with an Anglo accent, filled up the space, he had to ask what I meant, and his Greek was spoken in quick succession and the words hid behind his lips. He lit the cigarette and leaned back on the balcony wall. With the cigarette still in his mouth, his eyes still staring at me, he moved two fingers down to his crotch and peeled open his button fly, to reveal bright red briefs with blue piping. I looked down at his crotch, mute. Come on, he said, and then he took me into the room. He tried to kiss me, but I didn't like his mouth on me. The taste of beer and cigarettes took me back to the dark room days of my youth. I kissed his neck and there was a saltiness that was nice, so I focused on that. I tasted the brine on my lips. Clothes came off us. But in the middle of our interaction, I wanted to stop. There was no pleasure for me. In movies, books, art and talk amongst the community, the blond male Greek, with golden hair, was a trophy—the ultimate prize. Each of these boys, who became men, would be feted over, talked about, would let their melanin and hair colour do the talking. Since I was a child, one of the myths that went around the playground was that the reason the Greeks were dark was because the Turks had devoured all our bloodlines and had decided to make us impure. And there I was, going back to the golden fleece, and all I could sense and taste was not desirability for this man, but how he acted because others had told him he was desirable. The way he held his golden arms out, tiny gold hairs spun from straw. The way he leaned back, displaying the column of his throat to me, Adam's apple bobbing as he slid his tongue round the circumference of his mouth. This was a man, whose desires had been told to him, and once I understood that I could see there was nothing for me.

It was the look from that young male patient in the hospital bed that had reminded me of that Golden Greek man. I was walking to you and I had to shake my head a few times to come back to where I was. Reminding myself that my attendance there was as witness to your emergency. I kept walking past rooms with patients, in one was an older woman, and you gushed back into my brain. Where were you? There was another room where the air that flowed was neither cold nor hot, the temperature of the place felt completely unnatural. At the end of the hallway was the last room. There were four beds in there. Two of the beds were occupied. I walked into the room, to the bed at the end. You were lying there asleep, while machines bleeped. The walls were pale blue and the floors sterile. The bed had a chrome frame that was a rectangle around the mounds of your body.

Your breasts and stomach were hills under paper sheets. They heaved up and down with your breath. Your breath would stutter and regulate. At each stutter, my own breath would hold, and I imagined we were synchronised, that I might need to withdraw my own use of oxygen so you could use some. Under the dim light your skin was translucent, underneath your organs rustled. The mist coming out of your mouth reeked of your guts. I smelled the earthy scent of your bowels, mixed with bile and decaying teeth. I sat on a chair next to you, the rayon of my work uniform pressing against the vinyl. I went to run my hand through my hair but, as my fingertips touched the first strand, I realised my hair was still in pomade shine. I put the back of my hand on your forehead and your eyes stayed closed. A too-hot temperature. I left my hand there, the back of my palm felt rough on your creased forehead. The skin on your brow drained of its colour. I looked down on you, your eyes shut, frown lines arched in the middle of white tapered eyebrows. On the side of your eyes were crow's feet, deep set into your face. Your lips were a frosted colour and the marionette lines under your mouth seemed to be holding it open.

I leaned back on the chair. It was easy to rest my head on it and my eyelids slowly started to close. Each time they fell, my head would roll back, and under my eyelids in the darkness, I saw your face. Remembering where I was made me want to reach out for comfort. I sent an ex-partner a message, something insufferable, which he saw and didn't reply to. My phone was on the armrest, you kept swishing your head from side to side.

Involuntarily, my head rolled back again, eyelids dropping of their own accord. I started to think about the only other doctor I knew on a social level—a Greek one that worked in Italy. We had met the last time I was in Greece and I had been single. He came from a rural community named after the horses there. It was a small but historic place on the coast and near to Turkey and Macedonia. He had gold skin too, but he took no vanity in himself. There was always dark messy hair, which seemed a hairstyle he chose for convenience rather than any commitment to aesthetic. When we had first met in a district that was known for manufacturing ceramics, he was crouching on the steps of a raised park where anarchists had protests. There was something unforgivably casual about him and his nose, which was sharp and long, broken on its ridge, that made him extremely familiar to me. In fact, the first time I had thought about how typically Greek it was, I laughed. And after I realised that I had feelings for him, that he elicited a warmth in me, that nose was what I went back to. The thing that defined him. When I was in Athens, I had stayed in an area that was close to the centre of the city, notorious for its crime, refugees, and travellers. The hotel was less than mid-level but had a good breakfast buffet that I kept missing, with all the Greek things that I loved to eat like bitter black olives, yoghurts, and stone fruits. It was near a space that usually stood empty, making the place more desolate. But the space became a fruit market on Sundays, a place where farmers sold directly to vendors. When the markets were there, so were the beggars, Albanians, and Romani people, who wore clashing print fabrics and gave the impression of the old folk peasantries to a smog-filled Euro rubbish city.

Because it was all so much, I kept on going backwards to comforting memories. I had spent two weeks in Athens and there were periods when I couldn't leave my room. I was still taking antidepressants in the morning and antipsychotics at night. On those days, I found a channel on the television that played all the Greek folk pop songs, the ones that mixed up ancient pastoral odes with klarino, violins, and percussion. The voices I preferred were the dark rich smokers, men who compared the beauty of a lost love to the mountain fields. Or the yields of a harvest to the beauty of a woman's abundant hips and breasts. It was these songs that gave me access to your life. Those songs about the times in the villages. They conveyed your values. They taught about the agrarian and feudal world that you came from. With their help I imagined your world. The songs came into my room, filling it up and combining with the air conditioning, which I kept turning on and off, unsure if I wanted the cold or natural heat.

On my phone I would open an application that would allow me to see a grid of men around me. Athenian men were and are the most beautiful men. Most were under thirty and still had the effects of military service on their bodies. They kept slim, athletic, in that way that Southern European patriarchal cultures venerate men's beauty. On the gay grids it manifested in many forms. Some of the men used their beauty as a source of income, and those who paid were the ones that feted it.

One day I didn't feel like leaving the hotel, so I went upstairs to the roof. I looked over the decrepit Athenian city lit up by cheap lights, its half-built buildings never completed, and saw the Acropolis, perching above the place. She was looking over the city like a mother looking down on its child. And that was when I got my first message from the doctor. I asked for photos. One of the pictures was the standard photo of a man standing in front of a mirror. He was holding up his phone and it created a lens blur where the mirror was but showed a taut hairy body. The next image he sent was of him at a beachside village, sitting down at a table with a plate of lentils mixed with calamari. In the background were dirty white walls, pink doors and the sea stretching out. He was from the village of Drama, a town in Northern Greece. When he told me this, I knew that I would be safe with him. I knew from what you told me that we have generational relations through baptism with people from Drama. They are known to be the best people, in loving marriages that never divorce, and welcoming to all strangers.

On the day I left my room, I forced myself to make a day of it. I went to a museum and saw a large exhibition of a modernist painter, who was a communist and had spent his time painting scenes from the Greek Civil War. When I saw the representations of peasants and mortars, I thought about how the bombs had exploded in your childhood. In one painting there was an old loquat tree in front of a hut that had the roof caved in. Afterwards, I came back to the hotel and got myself ready for my date. I slicked my hair down and wore a black t-shirt.

Late, I walked through the city and felt particularly dapper. I was invisible to most Greeks but visible to the South Asian communities who mistook my hard hair and black t-shirt for a membership of the Greek Nazis and scuttled out of my way. Skirting the base of the Acropolis led me to the place where all the ceramics were made. The ceramics had only been there in ancient times and now it was a tourist trap filled with nightclubs and restaurants for the Eurorich. I found the doctor there. He came to me dressed in too-chunky shoes, denims, and a button-down. He didn't say it but he looked at me strangely for wearing shorts and a t-shirt at night with sandals, resigned to accepting it because I was a tourist. I could see he was a local and I thought on our first meeting how unimpressive he was. Average looks, taut body with a hooked nose. Nothing particularly charismatic, just earnest and open. He smiled easily, revealing strong teeth. There was a utilitarian aspect to him. I pointed to the Butcher Shop, a high-concept tourist restaurant. It served meat platters that foreigners mistook for Greek cuisine. The decorations were a simulacrum of the shabby chic of the islands, but I could tell the place wasn't authentic because the servers were nice. Doctor suggested we sit inside, I later found out he was embarrassed to be dining in such an establishment, especially when the Roma and street urchins kept asking for money. I ordered a meat plate. He wanted seafood and said it reminded him of eating in his grandparents' town of Drama. I asked him about his medical course. He said there was no future for him in Greece.

There seemed to be no future for anyone of a certain level of education in Athens.

We met up over the course of a few days. We went to gay nightclubs, and I bought him drinks. We never kissed but walked around at night talking. It was a wholesome coming-of-age experience, at my ripe age of thirty-something years old. We walked to the next place, and I put my hand on his bicep, happy to listen to him talking about his medical degree, even if it seemed like a rehearsed speech, something given to relatives. We went to a club named after a famous Greek porno star called Shamon. He told me that Michael Jackson used to sing about her. We descended some stairs, the music floated up and polluted us. Heady melodies that I anticipated would lead to eros in the air. We shared some retsina. Sitting next to each other, our legs touching. We walked to another club. I said that if I stayed with him, I could love him, that my feelings could grow. He said that he felt the same. The city became a house for him, and he showed me its rooms. One night we walked to the Tomb of the Unknown Soldier. I saw a child clinging on to its mother's velvet dress as she walked ahead. We parted ways soon after because I had to go to my next place. We never touched intimately. We never met up again. I went to the island of my ancestors, and he went to Seville to work. Sometimes I still think about his nose. That too-long hook. How he said he had feelings for me. Parts of me are comfortable with never fulfilling that relationship. All that emotion still stirs. I wonder if it has reached him from my hemisphere, especially when I am vulnerable, sitting next to you as you lie in a hospital bed. I have never thought about it until now.

I'm always next to you in times of crisis. Big and dramatic and gay moments. I'm always driving you places. Once in the car, I reminded you that you told me you didn't know if God exists. You looked beyond the window. Outside was darkness. You could have told me there was a little village out there with a family. Or that outside was Athens, and a young woman was coming out of girlhood. You could have told me that there was a hospital bed and I would've believed you. You wondered if indeed you ever told me that. You then said, with the easiest breath, sometimes I think God forgot about us because we were poor.

●

Just before the dawn you stir awake. You notice me and tell me to go home, I say I'm a big boy and can manage it, even though my eyes can't stay up. No matter how big someone is, a child never grows. I feel like I can easily be the height of your waist and you a column of thick black hair, hiding in your bedroom, crying in front of a jewellery box. My child's hand strokes your back, a bruise rising on the side of your face. But that bruise is steep like the mountains that cradle the village.

In your hospital room, it's not the bleach and sterilisation mixed with infected breath that stays in my nostrils, it's the plumes of Holiday cigarette smoke from when you sat at the kitchen table. From that time you dared me to try one. But then the menthol cigarette smoke changes into the Greek forest smell. Pine needles pressing against a handmade rug.

And when I look next to your hospital bed, a drip hangs with clear antibiotics, and there is a metal needle in your veins. The drip is your weeping eyes and those tears turn into the Greek rains that spank the side of mountains, they are the same ones that came during your baptism, hitting the limestone cliffs of the island, covering the village that you came from with a haze.

ACKNOWLEDGEMENTS

Rosie Dennis and UTP for their work on the performance text *Steps to Katouna* which informed this work.

The long-gone event called Men of Letters—the letter I read there made it into here.

Catriona Menzies-Pike for her work on the essay 'Mama becomes Medea' published in *SROB*—the ending of this book would not have been possible.

Professor Nicole Moore, Nigel Featherstone, UNSW Canberra and MARION for their support during my time as writer in residence.

The Alien, Antigone Kefala—a poetry book which helped me understand the images and feelings of a certain generation of settler migrants.

The Matchmaking of Anna, Pantelis Voulgaris—a film which helped me see and write Athens in the 1970s.

The Cookery of Lefkada, Evi L. Voutsina—an anthropological way of looking at my ancestral foods.

What Do Starving People Eat? The Case of Greece through Oral History—Dr Violetta Hionidou—thank you for letting me read this chapter and realise how famine foods are integral to our communities.

Diana, Katie, Helen, Giana, Amy—for the cousins group chat and helping me understand our family through stories.

Aunty Pelagia—for the lunches she hosted to tell me stories.

Anastasia Polites—for all the long discussions unpacking all this, her memories and most importantly the permission.